SHORT STORIES ARE NOT REAL LIFE

Also by David R. Slavitt

P O E T R Y

Big Nose
The Carnivore
Child's Play
Day Sailing
Dozens
The Eclogues and the Georgics of Virgil
Eight Longer Poems
The Elegies to Delia of Albius Tibullus
Equinox
Five Plays of Seneca
Ovid's Poetry of Exile
Rounding the Horn
Suits for the Dead
Vital Signs: New and Selected Poems
The Walls of Thebes

F I C T I O N

ABCD
The Agent (with Bill Adler)
Alice at 80
Anagrams
Cold Comfort
Feel Free
The Hussar
Jo Stern
The Killing of the King
King of Hearts
Lives of the Saints
The Outer Mongolian
Rochelle, or Virtue Rewarded
Ringer
Salazar Blinks

N O N F I C T I O N

Physicians Observed
Understanding Social Psychology
 (*with Paul Secord and Carl Backman*)
Virgil

E D I T E D

Land of Superior Mirages: New and
 Selected Poems of Adrien Stoutenberg

SHORT STORIES ARE NOT REAL LIFE

Short Fiction by

DAVID R. SLAVITT

1991

LOUISIANA STATE UNIVERSITY PRESS

Baton Rouge and London

Copyright © 1987, 1988, 1989, 1990, 1991 by David R. Slavitt
All rights reserved
Manufactured in the United States of America
First printing
00 99 98 97 96 95 94 93 92 91   5 4 3 2 1

Designer: Amanda McDonald Key
Typeface: Times Roman
Typesetter: Graphic Composition, Inc.
Printer and binder: Thomson-Shore, Inc.

Library of Congress Cataloging-in-Publication Data

Slavitt, David R., 1935–
    Short stories are not real life : short fiction / by David R.
Slavitt.
        p. cm.
    ISBN 0-8071-1665-3 (alk. paper)
    PS3569.L3S5 1991
    813'.54—dc20   91-18913
                                                         CIP

Some of the stories herein were published previously, as follows: "Short Stories
Are Not Real Life," in the *Michigan Quarterly Review* and subsequently in
Inside Magazine; "Spooky Stuff," "The Long Island Train," and "Something She
Touched," in *Inside Magazine;* "Conflations" and "Grandfather," in *Boulevard;*
"Instructions," in the *New England Review/Bread Loaf Quarterly;* "Parents'
Day," in *Shenandoah;* "To My Dying Day," in the *Texas Review.*

The paper in this book meets the guidelines for permanence and durability of the
Committee on Production Guidelines for Book Longevity of the Council on
Library Resources.⊗

For Susan and Fred Chappell

C O N T E N T S

Short Stories Are Not Real Life

So, I'm teaching.

I wanted to teach, but it is nothing like what I thought it would be. It isn't that coming in from the forbidding cold of the literary marketplace.[1] It is only a different kind of cold. I ought to have known, but then one never knows.

That's one of the main differences between literature and life. Literature is what you can make up, while life is the correction, what actually happens. Better writers than I have demonstrated their utter inability to live any more shrewdly than ordinary nonwriting mortals. But that is, as they say, another story.

What I imagined, I suppose I may as well confess, is some glossy advertisement of myself in tweeds, strolling about the gracious lawns of this ivied bastion of learning and civility. I wear the tweeds all right, but I feel like an impostor because my students and my colleagues are outfitted as urban guerrillas. And I spend almost as much time on the train or the bus as I do on the campus. The bus takes only half an hour longer and saves me ten dollars on each round trip. On the other hand, the bus takes me into the Port Authority Terminal and subjects me to that terrible walk from Eighth Avenue to Times Square on Forty-second Street.

On one of the marquees last week: *The Pink Clam*.

---

1. A reference to the annual publication of the R. R. Bowker Co.

If I were a better person, I wouldn't notice such things, or not so much as I do.

But that distressing block isn't any worse than the subway ride I have to take either way. *Apprenda Ingles*. Or, on the adjoining placard, *Apprenda terror*. They've got a selection of killers, rapists, and brutalizers for whom the police are looking, and they're willing to pop for a hundred dollars for information leading to the arrest and conviction, etc., etc.

Only a hundred? Is violence that common, that cheap?

But this isn't what you want to hear. This is your standard urban complaint and has nothing to do with life at the university (except, of course, that it does). I come out of the subway entrance after all, and pass through the tall and guarded gates of the university into a world that is supposed to be better and safer and isn't at all. I go to the building where I'm supposed to have my conferences, and I get into an elevator that is painfully slow and ugly. Sixteen thousand dollars a year they charge these kids, and the elevator looks as though it were from some project in an East Harlem slum. Its door takes an actual ninety seconds to close. The metal wall panels were in need of painting ten years ago, and the plastic shield over the fluorescent light has been removed, broken or stolen, so that there is a hideous glare. People in the elevator look in that terrible light as if they have some disease.

The bullpen in which I have these conferences is also awful, full of discarded typewriters on which people have left notes saying, "Broken. Dangerous. Do not use!" Most of the chairs are covered in leatherette and seem to be from dinette sets that have been broken up in domestic tragedies I don't choose to imagine. My little cubicle has one of those chairs, less extensively slashed than many, a wooden chair that I use, and an ugly wooden desk with two drawers, one of them locked and the other unclosable. In the unclosable drawer, one of my colleagues has stored a bottle of Almaden burgundy.

I guess it could be worse—MD 20/20 or Night Train, maybe.

What this large room looks like is the city room of some foreign-language newspaper, either the day before or the day after its bankruptcy.

I sit here, in my little cubicle, waiting for students to show up for their conferences. I will read their short stories. I will try not to let on that I don't much like short stories. But Ignoto and Ungar[2] teach the poetry courses, and novels are long and cumbersome and strenuous, which is another reason for my wanting to teach. Short stories are what's left. Short stories are what you can read aloud in class and then talk about for an hour or so. Which is what I do.

But what difference does it make? I mean, when I think about what I'm doing, teaching writing to young men and women, I have the nagging feeling that I'm probably doing them harm. It's like teaching them to go over Niagara Falls in a barrel. I never wanted any of my children to write. Why, then, should I encourage these kids? (I tell myself that it's very unlikely that any of them will actually succeed or persevere in the attempt . . . but that is not exactly soothing to my ruffled moral sense.)

On the bus into the City this afternoon, I was reading the T.L.S.[3] in which Robin Buss[4] wrote:

The novelist (or, for that matter, the writer on natural history) elaborates a context; the short-story writer highlights, and by lift-

2. *Ignoto* is Italian for "unknown." But there is a possible reference to David Ignatow, a poet on the faculty of the Columbia College of General Studies Writing Program. Ungar is probably imaginary.

3. The (London) *Times Literary Supplement*.

4. A reviewer for the T.L.S., not identified but perhaps related to John Butt, lecturer in Spanish at Kings College, and Colin Russ, lecturer in German at the University of Kent, both of whom appear in the same issue (4 October 1985).

3

ing something—an incident, a character—and making an entity
of it, implies its extensions.

Not bad, you know! It was in his (or her?) discussion of a
book of Daniel Boulanger's stories called *Les Noces du
Merle.* I am unlikely to read this book. It's in French, a
language I do not speak or even read very well, despite the
certification of this very university that I am proficient in
the *langue.* Not at all. I have looked up *merle,* and I'm able
to report that it is a blackbird or perhaps a water ouzel, but
why a blackbird (or water ouzel) should be getting married
beats the hell out of me.

But Mr./Mrs./Miss/Ms. Buss is on the right route
there, I thought, being myself on a Greyhound and not too
happy about it. In the seat behind me, a schizophrenic was
muttering and crooning to himself, which wouldn't have
been so bad if he hadn't occasionally surfaced into a kind
of sense, addressing some denizen of his memory or night-
mares and articulating all too clearly, "Come on, bitch,
where's the money? Give me the money, bitch! The money.
The money, bitch."

A black man in his early forties, I'd guess. And, dis-
tressingly, the bus was full so there was no possibility of
moving away from him, not for me nor for the woman in
the seat beside him, also black and quite uncomfortable.
She wore a hat with cherries on the brim, and she had a
Bible on her lap which she clutched either for divine protec-
tion or else to use as a weapon if it should come to that.

And what did I do? Nothing, of course. I mean, I
thought of going up front to report to the driver that there
was this raving lunatic on the bus, but what could the driver
have done? Put him off somewhere in the middle of the New
Jersey Turnpike and leave him to wander in traffic? The
woman with the Bible was free to complain herself if she
chose to do so. I had no more reason to interfere than
anyone else. And I was correct, I think. We got to New

York anyway, and no harm was done. Or no new harm, I should say.

But Buss was correct. Novelists build contexts, while short story writers work by synecdoche,[5] isolating and then implying some nimbus of meanings. It's a magic trick, really, a razzle-dazzle performance.

I open the school paper and read yet another account of a piece of distressing violence: some female undergraduate who accepted the offer from a young man wearing a college sweatshirt to help her carry her groceries from the supermarket back to her dorm. And, of course, she got attacked, tied up with wire, and her roommates were tied up . . .

I throw the paper away and open my briefcase, drawing out the brown manila envelope in which the short stories of my students are mixed in with departmental directives and printouts from the registrar's office that are inaccurate and out of date. I fish out one of the stories and read it.

There's a girl waking up, and the man with whom she spent the night is gone. His clothes are gone. But as she goes into the bathroom, she finds that the toilet seat has been left up. For a paragraph of fine writing, she looks in the mirror and considers her naked body.

Is this the writer's body? Is this a piece of literary exhibitionism? It is silly to suppose that the speaker in a short story has any particular relationship to the writer, but then these are students, and they may not know that rule. The odds are that this is all true, that this happened more or less the way it is written down. And if I have connected the name on the first page to the right face—and body—then the description is probably accurate, even to the large pink areolas.

The story is about the relationship between this girl and

---

5. The figure of speech in which a narrow term of reference is used for a wider one.

Hilda, her college friend who has been married and divorced and has a three-year-old son. They were roommates back in school, and they had a set of signals they used when one of them wanted the room to herself for a few hours, if she had a date she was thinking about going to bed with. Now, there is friction because the protagonist lives by herself and enjoys her freedom while Hilda has the kid to worry about. The protagonist baby-sits willingly enough, but Hilda appears to be jealous of the sexual freedom of her former roommate. What comes out, instead, is a weird and unpleasant jealousy of the friendship between the child and the narrator.

Not bad, really. It could be cut a little, here and there, but the basic structure is sound and the writing is efficient and graceful most of the time. A little flowery? But that could perfectly well be the character who's thinking and speaking this way. Certainly it's good enough to use in class. What I usually do is bring something along to talk about if there isn't anything from the work of the students that we can discuss.

John Leonard[6] passes by on the way to his cubicle, which is just beyond mine, and we exchange greetings. His left arm is in a sling, and I ask him who beat him up. I am making a joke, but it turns out that he really was beaten up. In the subway, on the way up to school a week ago, he saw a young woman being roughed up by a gang of four or five toughs, and he tried to stop them. They turned on him and bounced him around, literally and very hard, actually cracking his shoulder blade on one of the poles in the subway car.

"On the way to school?" I ask.

He nods, smiling ruefully.

"I mean . . . in the afternoon?"

"That's right."

6. Former book reviewer and columnist for the New York *Times* and for a time a member of the Columbia University College of General Studies faculty.

6

What can I say? I tell him I'm glad he's alive.

"Me, too," he says, and he goes on toward his cubby.

I'm distressed, of course, for his sake, but for mine as well. After all, that's the subway I take. I'd told myself that for little old ladies at three in the morning there was a certain risk, but for someone like me, six feet tall and hefty, at rush hour . . .

But would I have done what he did? I was at less risk on the bus, but then so was the woman the schizophrenic was bothering. It is an uncomfortable question, and either way I decide, I lose—on the grounds of cowardice or folly. Before I make my choice, my first student appears. Or, not so fast. An ex-student, as he announces himself.

He's something of a wreck already, a tall, shaggy kid with bad skin and a diamond stud earring in the lobe of one ear. He had shown me a competent if repellent story about young men and women in the East Village living in squalor and doing drugs, and there was a peculiar Raymond Carver[7] trendiness to the way he described his people and the things that happened to them, all with a weird flatness that a psychiatrist would call a lack of affect. And there was also a disturbing authority in the way he described his hero kicking off his shoe, removing his sock, and using it as a tourniquet so that he could inject heroin into a vein.

The writer has come by to say he can't make the class. At first I think that he means this evening's class, but he means the whole course. A conflict? Or is he dropping out of school entirely? He is unforthcoming and almost provocatively vague, but it was thoughtful of him to drop by and let me know. Otherwise, I'd have worried about him.

I will worry about him anyway.

He leaves, and the author of the story about the woman with the lovers and the jealous friend peeps around the par-

7. Author of *Cathedral* (Knopf, 1983).

7

tition. Yes, I'd remembered the right one, with the terrific complexion. And the pink areolas, too, I suppose. We discuss the story. Apparently I've got it wrong, was too quick in my reading, or too jangled. The mother really *is* jealous of the relationship between her friend and her little boy. I suggest that this is unlikely but that the unlikeliness is possibly useful for her. She can rewrite to make her story into something like the one I thought I'd read. And she can further complicate it by admitting a little jealousy on the part of her narrator toward the friend who has a child while she doesn't. Just a line somewhere about how her clock is running. "She must be in her late twenties?" I ask.

The writer is in her late twenties. She nods yes.

"Well, you'll think about it," I tell her. "Or we'll see what the class has to say. You don't mind if we do this in class?"

She doesn't mind. But she blushes. Stage fright? Or the business about the pink nipples?

She could omit that sentence, of course. But I can't tell her that. I couldn't tell the driver about the lunatic, and I couldn't have protected the girl in the subway.

Why Almaden? Why not whiskey in a flask? It's something to consider—not to leave in the desk drawer but to carry in my briefcase, along with the manila envelope.

I tell her that I think she's doing pretty well and that I'll see her in class in fifteen minutes or so.

She leaves, and another young woman is waiting to see me. She doesn't have anything to show me.

"Oh?" Usually, if they don't have anything, they just don't show up for conferences.

"It's been kind of a bad week," she says. And gradually she lets me know that she has had to move into a different apartment because somebody broke into the place she lived in before. "And, well, it was . . . very bad."

"You're all right, aren't you?"

8

"I am now. I was in the hospital for a couple of days."

"You were attacked?" I'm concerned but also thinking that this is crazy. All this in one day? But she's nodding. Does she want to talk about it? Does she want not to talk about it? I don't want to pry. I tell her that she can take her time and do something later on when she's up to it. It isn't a weekly performance, after all. Anybody who could write good stuff every week, reliably, wouldn't need the course.

I tell her to take it easy and ask if there's anything I can do. She shakes her head, but she smiles, acknowledging my good will.

We walk together across the campus to the classroom building. Small talk is not exactly appropriate, so I don't even try. I'm thinking that there's a Cheever story I've got in my bag that has a couple of nice moves in it. We can talk about that one. That and the pink nipples will get us through the two hours. But I'm also thinking that this is a terrible day and wouldn't fit into the conventions of short fiction. Too many coincidences. Too much, too much . . .

The class goes pretty much the way I expect, only we get the beginnings of a new story one of the young men has been toying with. He wants to see whether there are any possibilities he hasn't thought about. What catches my attention is that he's got footnotes throughout the story. It's an odd stylistic thing to do, and I ask about it. The only stories he's read are from *The Norton Anthology of Short Fiction*,[8] and he thinks all stories are set up this way.

I explain that this isn't necessarily so and show him the Cheever book, which has stories without footnotes. On the other hand, I find myself entertained by the idea. Why shouldn't stories have footnotes? At the very least, they

8. Edited by R. V. Cassill (Norton, 1978).

could be the parsley that decorates the platter and gives a certain authority to the *presentation*. Or a nice looniness.

Or innocence, which, on a day like this, seems particularly precious.

When the class is over, I put myself together, stuff the new material into my briefcase, and head toward 116th Street. Two of the students tag along with me, either in friendliness or because we are safer in a group. One of the students, a dark, rather chunky, but carefully groomed young woman, tells me about an episode last term when several members of one of her classes went together to the West End Bar for a few drinks. She left the bar a little before ten, went down into the 116th Street subway station, and got on a train. At 110th Street, two thugs got on and sat down near her, which wasn't in itself anything really alarming. She only began to worry when they got off at 34th Street, followed her to the ticket window of the Long Island Railroad, listened while she bought a ticket to Babylon, and then bought tickets to Babylon for themselves.

Now she was scared. She spoke to one of the trainmen and told him about the two young men who were following her. He asked where she was going, and she showed him her ticket. He told her not to worry and said he'd call the police. She got onto the train and waited, but no police showed up. The train pulled out, and the two young men were right there in the back of the car. They pulled into Babylon, and she got out, and they got out, and she began to walk faster, and they began to walk faster, and then a police car pulled up. The trainman had called the police after all, the Babylon police, of course, and they were just pulling into the station to meet the train. The two thuggy guys ran off, but it was a near thing. If those cops had been only a minute or two late, or if the trainman hadn't been so obliging as to make the call . . .

"Are you taking the subway?" she asks.

"Yes, but not just yet. There's a book I want to get, and I haven't had anything to eat."

There is an uncertain moment. I consider inviting the two of them to join me, but on the other hand, there are two of them, and I suppose they'll be safe enough, at least while they are together. Later on, the dangers will be greater. Besides, I really want to be alone. There is a Chinese restaurant down at 110th Street I like that one of my students told me about. It was closed down by the Board of Health for rats and has since reopened, but as the student said, that's a kind of recommendation. In the other Chinese restaurants around 110th Street, you have no idea how long it has been since the exterminator showed up or how many rats are running free. Besides, this one has a bar, and I can get a gin on the rocks, or even two, to cut through the accumulated residue of the day's dreariness. I like the Chinese place. The tables are close together, and one can eavesdrop, which is better than trying to read without spilling soy sauce on the book. And there is something reassuring and steadying about the Chinese waiters, fugitives from one great civilization and witnesses to the collapse of another, hustling pots of tea and platters of food when they have to, but mostly sitting around the large round table in the back, talking among themselves, laughing occasionally, but, more to the point, demonstrating an elegant ruefulness—which is, after all, what most short stories leave you with, isn't it? "Araby," "I'm a Fool," and "The Lady with the Pet Dog"[9] all come to a conclusion that would produce the expression and physical attitude of any of those waiters.

I drink my gin and wait for my hot and sour soup and beef lo mein. I also listen to a couple at the next table, very intense, probably graduate students. Or he is, anyway. He is wearing a denim jacket over a black T-shirt, jeans, and

9. Stories by James Joyce, Sherwood Anderson, and Anton Chekhov, respectively.

work boots. She is in a voluminous skirt and a tight black sweater. Nice figure. Hair almost black. A complexion that is smooth but running to olive, so that presumably her areolas are more brown than pink. The two of them are going through some crisis so serious that they can hardly talk about it. They do the things that people in short stories do, or people in short stories written by students: twiddling spoons and chopsticks, staring into a teacup as she is doing, or at the ceiling as he is doing, as if some answer might emerge there or at least the next line of dialogue. It is tempting to imagine him storming out of the restaurant. And she has no money, not a dime, and is embarrassed, but I come to her rescue, offering at least to lend her the money, which requires her to tell me her name and address. It is not hard to leap ahead, as I have been trying to get my students to do, leaving out the predictable and obvious details, the dumb novelistic information about how to dial telephones or put tokens in turnstiles, and arrive at her apartment, modest but neat, and, as a matter of personal preference and to avoid the cliché, devoid of insect life. Her areolas are, indeed, a lovely mocha, and her clam a glistening, healthy pink.

Nonsense. No such thing is likely to happen.

More likely is that they will leave together while I go alone down into the 110th Street station to get mugged by those toughs who are still there, frustrated after their attempt on my student that took them all the way out to Babylon and more dangerous than ever. My briefcase stolen, and my wallet, and my watch. My shoulder blade cracked like John Leonard's. I'll be lucky to get away with my life.

And what happens? What happens? It's a vulgar and gossipy question that a poet doesn't have to answer and that a novelist addresses in a very secondary way. But in a short story, we know that something is going to happen. We can tell, because we know that there's only a page or two left in the text, that a resolution is upon us of one kind or another. A moment of re-vision in which the writer makes his move. It can be some dumb piece of cuteness like "The Gift of the Magi,"[10] or it can be exquisite and perverse, a switch on our expectation that some sudden reversal is about to be effected, some transformation somehow imposed.

I am not set upon or mugged. I get back down to Times Square and across to the Port Authority Bus Terminal, make my way through the pimps and grifters and derelicts and schizophrenics. I don't see my friend from earlier in the day, but if I were to loiter a little and if my hearing were more acute, I have no doubt but that I'd be able to pick up the phrase that must be floating through the air: "Where's the money, bitch? Come on, bitch, the money!"

Without untoward incident, I board the bus and am even lucky enough to have two seats to myself so that I can doze on the way home. It is an uneasy sleep, the kind that would surely occasion a paragraph or two of dream material if life were a short story. But it isn't. Because I am on the bus, I remember the Buss piece in the T.L.S. and how novelists elaborate a context. Novelists and writers on natural history, I think it was, but then novelists are natural historians, whichever way you want to take that phrase. And life is not just sensations and assaults but a context, or a set of them, actually. Natural and unnatural histories. I am physically uncomfortable, gritty and exhausted after a trip into the City, but I have survived it, and I will return to my house, drink a glass of soda water, let the dog run in the yard, go into my study, where my wife will have put my mail on my desk, and then into the bedroom. She'll be asleep, but she'll know I'm home, and I'll get undressed as quietly as I can and get into bed beside her. I'll feel the warmth of her body, and the context of our lives will cover

10. Short story by O. Henry (William Sidney Porter).

us like the blanket with warmth and weight as if it were a physical object.

I have not been seduced. I have not seduced anyone. I have not been robbed or assaulted. Those are, like short stories, abrupt violations of life, and on the unreal island now behind me there is no way of distinguishing between the normal and the abnormal, the real and the unreal, or the text and the footnotes, for that matter. And I am not immune to those possibilities of dramatic reversal and loss. Nobody is. But my life is in that study and that bedroom. It is my childhood that you don't know about, and my parents' dreams for me, and mine for my children and grandchildren. None of that kind of thing is of interest to the writers of short stories.

The surrealist lights of the Bayonne refineries that I can see through the bus window look like a monstrous city, devoid of life but obviously full of energy, tanks of it, rows of gleaming pipes alive with it. There is a cracking tower with a pulsing plume of flame. One hardly needs to invent dream scenes; they leap out from all sides, or, as here, slip by at dizzying speed. I close my eyes but don't sleep. Instead, I think of my students, sad and brave, more or less blessed or afflicted with talents for writing and living. At the moment, they are occupied with short stories and experiences, but someday they may go on to novels and lives.

Which will be, I hope, mostly dull and mostly happy.

Spooky Stuff

He was a friendly acquaintance, the kind of fellow you might drift over to at a cocktail party because he's not, after all, a stranger. Or greet, even with warmth, on a chance encounter in a railway station as someone to talk with on the trip into the city. But he knows and you know, every time you part, that your promises to call each other for lunch won't be kept.

Still, in that limited way, it was pleasant to recognize Fred's face and odd slouch. I waved, and he tucked his paper under the arm that was carrying his briefcase so he could wave back—a fairly elaborate maneuver, actually. He was wearing a tweed suit I hadn't seen before and was looking rather professorial. Of course, we would ride together. He apologized about having some work to do on the train, but I didn't mind, and I told him so.

What I did mind, I realized, as I watched him pull his pipe from his pocket and fuss with it, was that I was now committed to the smoker. I caught myself hoping the train might be crowded, that there wouldn't be two seats together, and that I could make another of those empty promises to get together soon and then go find a seat in a non-smoking car.

We found two seats together, though, and settled in. Fred lit his pipe and puffed away to get it going, and we made small talk for a while before he opened his briefcase and pulled out a set of legal papers. I opened my *Times* and started to

read. It was unsatisfactory, but it would be over soon
enough.

Fred surprised me, though, by putting his papers aside,
turning to me, and saying, "You know, a funny thing happened to me."

"Yes?"

"It was about a month ago. And I can't understand it."

"All right," I said, half interested and half alarmed. I
was not the kind of person to whom he would be likely to
confide intimate secrets, was I? I wanted to go back to the
moment when all I had to worry about was being in the
smoker.

"I'm not a genealogy nut," he said. "I don't like those
people much who worry about ancestors. But my grandfather and my grandmother were divorced. I never met my
grandfather, actually. My grandmother remarried and had
another set of children. One day I found myself wondering
about whether my grandfather had remarried also and had
other children. This wasn't any pressing problem, but . . .
interesting. A small loose end. I tried to put it out of my
mind, mostly because I have that contempt for genealogy.

"But then I realized that I have a cousin, Stanley, who
lives in Minneapolis and who is ten years older than I am. I
thought I could call him up and ask, and he'd be able to tell
me whether our grandfather ever remarried."

He stopped, did more things with tamping and relight-
ing, and made a cloud of smoke that wasn't as bad as it
might have been. At least it wasn't that awful sweet kind of
tobacco.

"So you found a whole new set of relatives?" I asked,
prompting him to go on.

"No. I didn't call. I decided it was silly. I hadn't talked
to Stanley for . . . it must be twenty years. And nothing
new had happened, so there wasn't any reason for me to be
interested now. It's just that this question had occurred to
me. I was afraid of sounding ridiculous, I guess. I decided

16

not to call. But once I'd decided that, it should have gone away, but it wouldn't. It kept on bothering me. So on Monday morning I admitted to myself that I couldn't stand it anymore and I did call him. I called his office in Minneapolis and got his son, Jack. Who told me that Stanley had died two days ago. The day I'd first thought of calling him. After twenty years!"

I told him I guessed it was just coincidence. Which was, oddly enough, what he wanted to hear. The spookier explanations that sprang to mind were all embarrassing, and they inevitably smacked of cheap fiction or even cheaper spiritualism. They were violations of good taste, as out of place as a gaudy hand-painted tie would have been with Fred's tweed suit. And I believed what I was telling him. The only such premonition or intuition I've ever had didn't even involve a human being. I once had a dream, when I was at school, about the death of my dog, and the next day I called home to learn that the dog had, in fact, died of some sudden virus. I hadn't even known he was sick, but that dream—a vivid dream in which I was taking his body out to the curb in a dented galvanized garbage can—had told me, perhaps at the very instant of his death, what was happening.

But this hasn't been reliable. People have died, people I've loved dearly, and I haven't had any inkling at all until the phone rang and the terrible news came spewing forth in the ordinary way.

Fred went back to his legal papers and I started the crossword puzzle. It was odd, I supposed, that my program in the city that day included a dinner with my cousin Lenny, whom I don't see very often. But that wasn't very much of a coincidence, was it?

Lenny and I met at a Chinese restaurant he likes on Broadway in the nineties. I'd asked him to decide where we'd eat because I'd worried that an expensive place would be more than he could afford, while a cheap one might be insulting. Lenny is in fabrics, in positions and capacities that change from time to time. He has put on weight, and he has a beard, but it makes him look more Cuban than Jewish. We'd seen each other at Aunt Molly's funeral a couple of months before, and we'd agreed, in the way relatives do at funerals, that we ought to get together under more cheerful circumstances. Lenny had then called me a couple of times to ask about having dinner sometime when I was in town. How could I refuse? After all, it had been less than a year since the funeral of his father, my Uncle Ben. And Lenny's mother, Aunt Ida, wasn't well. I'd looked on my calendar, found a date in the suitable middle distance, and offered it. And here I was. Well, in two or three hours I'd be back on the train.

Lenny isn't so hard to take, though. He's just a little depressing. So was Uncle Ben, for that matter. Unsuccess dogged him throughout his life. I have no actual proof, but my guess has always been that both my father and Uncle Harry helped Uncle Ben out from time to time with sums of money that were called loans out of politeness.

Over our dumplings Lenny and I talked. He talked about his father: "Do you remember at the funeral the rabbi calling him a 'sportsman'? That was my idea. I wanted something in there that was actually about him, and you couldn't just say he was a card player and that he followed the horses. So I figured that 'sportsman' would sound dignified enough for the synagogue.

"He never made a lot of money," Lenny told me, "but he had a good time. I hope he had a good time, anyway."

"I hope so," I said.

We went through the family, mentioning various names and exchanging tidbits of news. I told him that I'd heard that Uncle Harry's vision was going. He couldn't read anymore, which was upsetting.

"I'm sorry to hear that," Lenny said. "We never got on well, though, that part of the family and ours."

"Oh? Why not?"

He told me the story. I knew—or thought I remembered—that Uncle Ben had been in the liquor business for a while. He'd worked for a wholesaler in some capacity or other. And, as Lenny now informed me, there was a moment when Uncle Harry had called Uncle Ben to come up to Peekskill because there was a liquor store he knew about that was for sale. Uncle Ben came trotting up, all excited. He could move out of the Bronx and live in Westchester. He could have his own business. "He was already there, in his mind, running that store," Lenny told me, offering me the last of the dumplings.

"Let's divide it," I said. "What happened?"

"Well, they went to look at the store, and it was okay, and the books were good, and the place was doing good business. And the price they were asking was okay. The owner had had a heart attack or something and he couldn't run it anymore. And Uncle Harry asked my Pop, 'So, how much money have you got? Can you afford it?' And my Pop told him what Uncle Harry had to have known from the beginning, that he didn't have any money at all. He'd assumed Harry was going to lend him what he needed and that he'd pay it back over the years.

"It was a joke. A terrible joke. Pop never talked to him again."

"That's odd," I said. "It's not in character."

"You think Harry's too nice?" Lenny asked. "My Pop walked away. He walked in the rain to the Peekskill train station and took a train back to the city."

"Terrible," I agreed. "But it still doesn't fit with Uncle Harry. He's too crude. He's the kind of guy who likes pratfalls and pies in the face. This was too elaborate. I mean, if it was a joke, it had to be thought out ahead of time and then played all day with a straight face. That isn't Harry's style. He could laugh at somebody else doing a thing like that, maybe, but he couldn't do it himself. I think it was a misunderstanding somehow."

"How?"

"I don't know," I said, and I tried to invent some plausible story. "Everybody says that he was a kind of a Neanderthal whom Aunt Helen just barely managed to tame. Maybe she told him what to do, to help your father buy the store, but she didn't spell it out because she thought it was obvious and didn't need to be said. And then, afterwards, when he got home, it was too late, impossible by then to fix, because your father's feelings had been hurt and he'd have refused."

"You think he's that much of a dummy, though?" Lenny asked.

"It's a tough call," I said. "Which way would you rather have it—that he was stupid or cruel?"

"I don't think it matters much," Lenny said. "Life is too short."

I agreed, and we opened our menus to consider our choices for the rest of the meal.

On the train going home—why is it that they find especially depressing cars with garish lighting and ancient seats upholstered in worn plush, as if to suggest that taking a train as late as this isn't quite nice?—I found myself considering the problem Lenny had posed. I figured it would not be difficult simply to call Uncle Harry and ask him what had happened fifteen or twenty years ago with that liquor store in Peekskill.

But of course I couldn't. That would be impossible. What could Uncle Harry tell me? That he'd been cruel? Or stupid?

Uncle Harry is an old man, well into his eighties, and he was never easy to talk to. He was one of those casualties of immigration, a man for whom the goal of success in the new country became such an imperative that he was willing to sacrifice everything else in order to achieve it: civility, refinement, the capacity to enjoy any of the rewards of his labors. He had come over here as a young boy, had learned English, had gone to work making false teeth, and eventually had bought the business, which developed into a chain of dental laboratories. And after a time he'd discovered that there was as much money to be made in the manipulation of real estate as in the primary job of making crowns and bridges. At first he only bought buildings where he could start new branches of his business, but then he began buying just for speculation. Small buildings and shares of larger ones. Pieces of shopping centers and malls. He made a lot of money, but never enough for him to feel comfortable. My father told me about how he would go around inspecting properties he owned or properties he was thinking about buying, and always with an unlit cigar stub in his mouth— because it lasted longer that way.

He probably could have helped his younger brother and sisters, my father and Aunt Molly and Aunt Ida, more than he did. But I never had the sense that he was mean. Not mean enough, anyway, to have pulled a stunt like the one Lenny had described. And yet I could not doubt what Lenny had said. Something like that must have happened. He had told me about it as one speaks of one of those rare cataclysmic events. It had done something to Uncle Ben, destroying his last illusion of competence or his last hope that something good might yet come to him in this life. It had confirmed him as a loser.

Unreasonable, of course. What possible reason could there have been for Uncle Harry to treat his brother-in-law that way? With whatever intention or inadvertence, though, people do things like that to each other, and they cannot be undone.

When I got home, tired and gritty from the trip, I

glanced at the mail and was surprised to see the return address of an old friend, a classmate at school, my roommate, in fact, at the time I had my dream about the death of that cocker spaniel. We exchange letters every few months. It is something of a pose. We could make phone calls. But it is pleasant to pretend that we are characters in an epistolary novel and to take the time and trouble to commit words to paper. Oliver teaches English in a university in the Southwest, and he has always had a playfulness about him. We laughed a lot together back in school. We still amuse each other.

There was nothing playful about this letter, though. In his tiny delicate script, he wrote:

Dear Bill,
Something weird has happened.
You remember Mary, of course. I had her picture on my dresser in our room. The girl of my dreams, etc., etc. I got a postcard from her on Friday, mailed several months ago when she was in Paris but arriving here, as those things will, well after the return of the traveler. I telephoned her to thank her for thinking of me, and I was told she had died. Of an aneurysm. That morning! Forty-seven years old!
I am saddened, as you can imagine. But also disturbed. This is spooky stuff!
Please write——

Love to all,
Oliver

He had wanted to marry her. I think they were actually engaged for a while, but then she ran off with some Texas millionaire. Oliver was not crushed by this, but rueful. Philosophic. He said at the time that he might very well have done the same thing if he'd been Mary. And that there were, in those long novels he taught, always more chapters. More vicissitudes. Perhaps her husband would die, and he could yet marry her and retire. But that never happened.

Still, as he'd said, this was spooky stuff. And spookier still, there was the coincidence of Fred's story that morning.

Was someone trying to tell me something? What was it that I was being told?

I had a dream that night, the kind of dream that psychiatrists dismiss, calling them junk dreams, in which the brain is clearing out the debris of the day's experience. But this was very vivid and convincing.

It was about Uncle Harry and Uncle Ben, and I could see them on their trip to Peekskill. The interesting thing was that this dream was like a short story, a study in point of view. I was limited only to Uncle Harry's head. But that was the right head to be in, for I could see, as clearly as Harry, the blood on the walls, the smashed liquor bottles, the legs of the corpse protruding from behind the counter.

And in my dream Uncle Ben can't see it, doesn't react, is blinded by his desire to own a business and be a success.

Uncle Harry has learned to trust his hunches. Real estate is a business that relies to some degree on those irrational promptings, and Harry's success has taught him to pay attention to them.

What can he do? Tell his brother-in-law that if they buy the store he'll die there, that he'll be dead on the floor with his legs sticking out from behind the counter?

Harry knows perfectly well that Ben won't believe it, not for a moment. Harry knows that Ben will think he is being trifled with, toyed with. But the alternative is that Harry will put up the money and that Ben will die. And Ida will be left a widow. And Lenny will be fatherless. Better that Ben should be alive in the Bronx than dead on the floor in Westchester . . .

So he plays dumb and goes through that awkward scene in which he asks Ben whether he has the money. And Ben says no, he was expecting Harry to lend it to him.

And that is the end of the relationship. From then on,

there's only hatred, not just until the day Ben dies but afterwards, from his son, too.

I woke up. I sat up in bed, absolutely sure of the truth of my dream.

I thought I might call Uncle Harry and ask him. Yes, in the morning, I could do that.

But I remembered Fred's story, and I realized that if I made that call, I might very well hear the news that Harry was dead.

Call Lenny, then, to tell him about my dream? No, not him, either.

Dumb, I admit, but why take the risk? If Harry could do so much for Ben, couldn't I do this one small thing? Couldn't I keep my curiosity to myself?

We learn to live with uncertainties.

The answers, if there are any, will come clear soon enough.

Happiness

A bunch of the guys were sitting around the table, drinking and telling stories . . .

Easy to say, but how often does such a thing actually happen? I asked myself that, realizing that the question itself was that of an outsider, which in a way I was. I had a wife, after all. Back at the motel, she had taken her cold pill and was asleep by now. But she had not wanted to keep me from participating in any of the reunion festivities.

These were classmates. Not friends, really, although I had known a couple of them twenty-five years ago, when we'd been undergraduates. But not intimately. And we hadn't kept up. The others were just classmates, people I'd never known, whose faces I would not even have been able to pick out of a crowd. Their tailoring, though, was familiar.

On the other hand, the thing I'd discovered about this reunion that pleased me was that you could risk encounters with strangers. It wasn't like a resort or a cruise where you have to be careful about what gestures you make. Here, you weren't likely to find actual barbarians. And more often than not, these hitherto unknown classmates turned out to be interesting, lively fellows. A decent crowd!

The admissions office, a generation ago, may have made its mistakes and probably had its prejudices, but given their aims, they hadn't done badly.

My wife had taken one of the yellow school

buses back to our room. The college had provided these to shuttle between the Lawn Club and the inn so that none of us had to bother with cars or brave the drizzle. And I'd stayed on for the mellow dwindling of the evening. In the larger dining room, the one with the dance floor, there were still the husbands and wives, dancing or talking about their kids, some of whom were already enrolled as freshmen or would be applying for admission next year. But in the corner of this smaller room, there was a large table, all male, the way things used to be before coeducation. A bunch of guys sitting around a table, drinking and telling stories.

They weren't all bachelors. Some were married but had come up alone. Henry's wife, for instance, had had foot surgery earlier in the week. Others were recovering from divorces. Or not recovering.

Chester Mapes was saying, "I expected that my wife would be unpleasant about it. I mean, if we'd been able to get along, we wouldn't have been going through this divorce business. What surprised me was how other people behaved. People I'd thought were friends, our friends but my friends as much as hers, either took sides—hers mostly—or just dropped both of us."

"You just throw away your address book and start fresh," Bill Gorman said, swirling his ice cubes around and around. "Everybody does that."

I hadn't known Gorman and wouldn't have known his name but for the blue-and-white button on his lapel proclaiming it and our class numerals. I had one on my lapel, too.

From the next room there was the sound of the band, which had finished its break and was playing slow fox-trots for the couples, our classmates and their now-matronly wives, or their new wives, some of them startlingly younger, or women who weren't their wives but were just up for the reunion weekend.

Mapes agreed with Gorman in a general way, but he insisted that what had happened to him had been different. "It was weird! There were friends of my wife who turned me into a project. I was a hobby of theirs. It became a game."

He had to explain what he meant. "They watched me. It may have begun accidentally, when one woman saw me at a restaurant or a party somewhere and recognized me— and I either didn't recognize her or didn't even see her. But she knew who I was and perhaps knew the woman I left with or was able to find out who she was. Now, this had nothing to do with my divorce. I mean, Corinne and I were already living apart. But this friend of Corinne's found out the name of the lady I was seeing and looked up her number and maybe just as a joke called her up and told her all about what kind of a monster I was and what peculiar sexual tastes I had. Some of it was just invented. Some of it was exaggerated from stuff she'd heard—I guess from Corinne. Exaggerated and twisted. And of course this woman didn't want to see me anymore.

"No huge loss, maybe. Annoying, but . . . I can see it as a kind of practical joke I might have played myself if I'd been in Corinne's friend's place. But they decided that this was great sport. It was good enough to do again. So they started watching me. All the women in Corinne's support group—or whatever they call those things—began spying on me."

"You're kidding," somebody said.

"Or exaggerating," somebody else suggested.

"It wasn't all the time," Mapes admitted. "It was just when they felt like it. They were bored, maybe, and they didn't have anything else to do. So they decided to go spy on Chester. They found another woman I was seeing, and they called her, too, and told her I was impotent. Not always, but after the first couple of times. And they sent her a dozen Chap Sticks."

We laughed at that.

"Sure, it's funny. But it wasn't so funny when this woman decided she wouldn't see me anymore either."

"She believed them?" somebody asked. "Couldn't you just prove to her that they were wrong?"

"I could have. I never had any problem that way—I mean, no more than anyone else. When I wasn't drunk or exhausted, I never had any problem. But if you have to prove each time that there isn't any problem, then you might eventually develop a problem. So I started to worry that I might start to worry about it. And she just didn't want the hassle of women calling her to ask if old Chester was still getting it up for her or if the novelty was wearing off. And it kept on going. For months. In New York, or Chicago, or Washington, or L.A., it would have been different, but Indianapolis is a small town, basically. There are only so many places you can go."

"So what did you do?" I asked.

"The wrong thing, of course. I asked Corinne to stop it. Or to have it stopped. But she wasn't doing it. These people were friends of hers, but they'd kept her out of it. So when I asked her to have it stopped, she could be lofty and sympathetic and tell me how much she disapproved of it, but there wasn't anything she could do. And she was enjoying the hell out of it."

We were naturally sympathetic, and we all agreed that this had been extraordinary. And very bad. But Bill Gorman then suggested that there were worse things than spite. "The worst is when the intentions are kind and generous and you see through that to something else . . ."

Gorman wasn't being very clear, and he knew it. He hesitated. Then, almost visibly, he decided, what the hell, we weren't people he saw all the time. We weren't friends exactly, but both more and less. If he couldn't talk to us, he couldn't talk to anyone. So he told us the story of what had happened to him, perhaps fairly recently. "There was this gorgeous woman I met at a convention, a real knockout. Tall and . . . 'statuesque' is what we used to say. And very smart. An executive in a company we do business with now and then. I'd known her for a couple of years, and we'd flirted, the way people in the same business do. Nothing serious, but not entirely without significance, either. If she was ever to feel in the mood and want company, I was sure as hell willing. That's how these things happen, I think. You let them know you're a player, and you wait, and sooner or later you find yourself in some strange city, and she's just broken up with a man and is looking around, not for a new roommate, maybe, but for somebody to console her. Or maybe just to use to erase the other guy a little. Anyway, I'd established myself there on her list of possibilities, and we laughed at each other's jokes, and there we were . . ."

He paused and looked around. We felt a bit uncomfortable—I did, anyway—partly curious and partly embarrassed by this candor of his. How ready were any of us to expose ourselves this way?

"But you know that line about how the worst I ever had was wonderful?" Gorman continued. "It's not true. I mean, this was wonderful, but it was also terrible. We got into bed, and she suddenly produced from her purse this little bottle of Johnson and Johnson's baby oil that she carried around with her, and she rubbed it all over me, which was wonderful, except that I realized it takes a lot of practice to get that good at something, which wasn't so wonderful. I guess what bothered me was that she was more eager to please than she needed to be. And as I thought about it, I got depressed because what I was seeing and feeling and benefiting from had to be the result of a lot of experience. Some of which hadn't been so good, I thought, although that may have been a bit sentimental."

"Or a bit prudish, perhaps?" someone suggested.

"That's what I told myself," Gorman said. "But I'm afraid I had it right. Later on, when it was over and we were about to fall asleep, I noticed her taking a handful of pills, and I asked what they were. She told me they were Desyrel—to keep her from being suicidal. Nice? It made me feel like . . . a monster. I'd rather have had my ex-wife's friends making that accusation. At least I could laugh at it or shrug it off somehow. But if you're making the accusation yourself, it's harder to dismiss, you know? And she was so gorgeous. The worst of it is, I don't know but that I wouldn't do exactly the same thing again. It hasn't changed me or made me a better person. Nothing."

A few of us went over to one of the service bars to get fresh drinks—at this stage of the evening brandy or neat whiskey. When we came back to the table, Stu Kerner was talking, either answering some question or just volunteering the information about what his life was like and how things were with him. He had a wife he loved and two kids, and he was perfectly happy with his life, he said, but he wasn't a saint. "And everybody gets restless. You get to thinking what you might have missed or might be missing. Not so much other women, but other parts of yourself that those women might have elicited, you know? And then it's so easy these days, with all these women who don't want entanglements and who have careers, who actually prefer married men because we're not a threat. It's so common that they're writing about it in women's magazines—which is a little depressing. You don't like to read how your life is trite."

He lit a cigar with a wooden match from a gold match case. He noticed that I was admiring it.

"Yes," he said, "it is nice, isn't it?"

From the way he looked at the match case before putting it back in his pocket, I guessed that it had been a present either from the wife or from the career woman.

"Have you ever read Chekhov's story 'The Woman with the Dog'?" he asked. "It's a love story. These two people meet at Yalta, and they're there alone, although each is married. He seduces her. It's great. And then she gets a telegram and has to go back to her husband, and that's great, too, because it saves him the problem of disentanglement, he thinks. But he goes back to Moscow or St. Petersburg, I forget which, and he can't stop thinking about her. He just can't get her out of his mind. So he goes off to whatever provincial city she lives in, and he finds some way to meet her—I think in a theater. She's horrified to see him because she hasn't been able to forget him, either. She begs him to go away. And he says he will, if she'll come to Moscow to meet him. And she promises that she will.

"And then you figure, because it's a short story, there's going to be some sort of a twist. That it will all blow up and their lives will be ruined. They won't like each other anymore. Or his wife will find out, or her husband. Some disaster. But what happens is that they're perfectly happy, and they can only meet a couple of times a year for a few days. And they live like that for the rest of their lives, in a kind of torment . . . And that's the twist! That's the surprise ending! Or the punishment. And it's the worst ending that Chekhov could devise for them."

"Oh?" somebody asked.

"Yes," Kerner said.

We waited for him to tell us what had happened to him, or at least how the Chekhov story bore on his own experience, but he didn't say anything more. He puffed on his cigar and announced that he needed a freshener. Then he got up and went out to the bar.

"He comes to New York once a month or so," Gorman said, after Kerner left us. "He used to call us sometimes, and he'd show up for dinner or even spend the night, but he hasn't called lately. I guess that must be why."

Gorman and Kerner, I recalled, had been roommates back in school.

When Kerner returned to the table, we waited again for him to continue. It was awkward. But then, mercifully, Kevin O'Grady asked Kerner if he'd ever heard the story about Madame de Gaulle. "It's as much to the point as that Chekhov story, I think."

Kerner hadn't heard it, nor had any of the rest of us, so O'Grady told it: "Madame de Gaulle came to America once on some state visit, and there were all these reporters who showed up to interview her at a press conference at the French embassy. One of the reporters asked her what was the most important thing in life. And without a moment's hesitation, she told the reporters, 'The most important thing in life is a penis.' Of course, they were shocked. Couldn't believe their ears. And they were right, too. Because what they'd heard was her heavy French accent. What she'd thought she was saying was 'happiness,' but if you drop the aitch and scramble the vowels and the stresses a little, that's where you come out: 'ap-PI-ness!'"

We laughed. And from the next room, we heard the sound of the band playing another sentimental number. The couples in there were happy, we supposed. Or at least pretending to be. In here, there was a kind of rueful brotherhood that was momentary if not actually illusory. Five years from now, at the next reunion, which of us would be out there? Which of them would be in here with us? Which of us, for that matter, would still be alive and well and able to come back this way to drink and smoke cigars, sit around the table and tell stories of how our lives had gone, what we regretted, and what we still wished for?

I think of those men, not close friends, just classmates—which in a way is even better—decent people, good fellows, bravely bearing up as they go about their business and pursue their pleasures, sometimes bewildered, but trying not to be too dreary about it. I remember how Gorman raised his glass and made a wise-ass toast: "Gentlemen, 'ap-PI-ness!"

And O'Grady, responding with elegant formality, stood and proposed, with the fervor of the Free French in World War II, "Vive de Gaulle!"

Conflations

If you can get far enough into the distance,
you approach a vanishing point.

Well, not really. It's only theoretical, after all,
a trick someone worked out in the Renaissance
that makes perspectives look right. Because wher-
ever you are, that's the foreground, and you never
get to that wonderful, faraway place where lines
all come together.

Or that's what I used to think. I'm not so sure
anymore. I'm not so sure of anything these days.

I am in a large restaurant on the Connecticut
shore, and everyone in the room is family. Or
friends of family. The fact that I hardly know most
of these people is not at all surprising. We are
hardly a large clan, but we aren't what anyone
would call close-knit.

No, it isn't a dream. It could pass as one,
maybe, but this is a perfectly matter-of-fact event,
my uncle's eighty-fifth birthday party. And my at-
tendance is almost accidental. I had a lecture to
deliver not far from here, and I called up a week
or so ago to announce to my cousin that I'd be in
the area. I see my cousin Bob and his wife, Greta,
maybe once every couple of years. They were
glad to hear from me and told me about the birthday party. They hadn't wanted to impose, but
they'd be delighted if I'd come, they said.

So I came. I'm here. And I'm feeling a little
like an impostor. I mean, I'm a legitimate relative,
but the imposture is that we're the kind of family
that gets together for these occasions. We do, I
guess, but mostly for funerals and, if we're com-

fortable about them, our children's weddings. What have
we got in common?

Bobby owns racehorses, for God's sake. There are
silks now with the family colors. Too rich for my blood!
Except, of course, that it is my blood. We're first cousins.
And Bob's father, my uncle Abe, is pleased that I'm here to
help celebrate his birthday, not for my own sake so much as
for my late father's. If I am here, his late brother is not
absolutely absent.

I am happy enough to serve in that capacity.

Several of us are standing around at the bar, waiting for
the birthday boy to show up, and I'm thinking about my
uncle and my father, and how different their lives were and
yet how much alike they were, and he appears. When my
turn comes to greet him and wish him happy birthday, I tell
him he is looking good, as indeed he is, and I ask him how
he is feeling—a perhaps indelicate question to put to a man
on his eighty-fifth birthday. He holds out his hand, yaws it
slightly from side to side, and says, "Beh-meh," which is
Yiddish for mezzo-mezzo. Just as my father would have
said and done. I grab another drink.

I am the one who is supposed to represent my father
for him, not the other way around.

But that's how things are sometimes. And the costs are
tough to calculate. All I am really reacting to is his terrific
tailor, who's made him look impressive. His dark blue suit
has been fitted perfectly, so that he looks trim and fit. My
uncle has always dressed well. So did my father. Their father was a tailor, and they learned about clothing. It isn't
just having the money to spend; you also have to know what
you're doing. Not that either of them would ever actually
talk about such things. They weren't ashamed of knowing, but they weren't exactly comfortable or happy, either.
I envy them that knowledge, but that's because I don't
have it.

A cousin shows up, not mine but my uncle's and my

father's. He, too, is named David. And he must be . . . ninety-four? Ninety-five? We greet each other, and I identify myself for him. "I'm Sam's son," I tell him.

"Ah, Sam," he says, sighing.

He doesn't hear too well. Or see too well. But up there in the middle nineties, the standards change. I am prepared to make allowances and am feeling . . . decent. I am a good boy. Fifty years old, and I am having a flash of that old feeling of doing the right thing and getting approval from family.

As we exchange remarks, however, it becomes clear to me that my cousin David—first cousins once removed, I guess, is what we are—has conflated me and my father. "Ah, Sam"—that wistful remembrance has prompted Sam's return. As far as he is concerned, I am my father. He asks me about my son, the writer.

And there I am, with a son who is a disappointment, not having gone to law school but having deliberately chosen a life of uncertainty and self-indulgence. I know the lines, having heard them often enough. Still, I am not going to put myself down. "He's doing well," I say to him, meaning that I am.

"I am glad to hear it," he says, nodding slowly and offering me consolation for having an errant child.

He doesn't have what one of my children once referred to as Old-timer's disease, but neither is he altogether here. He is there, at that vanishing point, where all those lines and planes come together at last. Fine for him, but he has dragged me along with him.

I am about to ask after his children and grandchildren, but he is snatched away to pose for photographs. He is a physician, or used to be. My uncle and my cousin are both lawyers, as my father was. My children—a doctor, a lawyer, and a management consultant—are the children my father would have liked to boast about on occasions like this.

The picture taking goes on for quite a while. It is one

of those odd occasions that will have its primary existence as much in the fixity of an album's pages as here, in this room, in this blur of time. My uncle and his cousin David. My uncle and my cousin Bob. My uncle and his partner, who is ill. Who is dying, I am told. Some degenerative disease I have never heard of but which is one of those slow destroyers of the muscles and nerves.

Another vanishing point.

There are more arrivals, this time of some people I know. My aunt Tady, who is Abe's and my father's sister, and her son, my cousin Louis, show up. Louis does public relations for politicians, and he has an elegant cynicism and a fund of funny stories I like to listen to. I think—as I have always thought—Louis is a good kid, and then I catch myself because Louis is in his forties.

His father, my uncle Carl, used to clown around and scare my sister and me when we were little, doing a Lamont Cranston routine to which he'd added an irrelevant but still impressive Frankenstein's-monster walk: "Who knows what evil lurks in the hearts of men? The Shadow knows!" And then he'd do the stiff-legged walk and poke whoever was closer in the belly button with an extended forefinger.

He's dead now, and unless Louis is inventing another amusing tall story, Uncle Carl's got a pack of cards with him in his coffin, on the off chance that he'll find a few players in the other world.

My sister isn't here. She's down in Washington. She would like to have been invited and feels left out, but my guess is that Bob and Greta were being considerate and didn't want to impose and drag her all the way up to Connecticut just for a dinner.

She'll get invited to the funerals—Tady's, which will be in a year or two if the doctors are right, and Abe's, which can't be a lot farther off. At eighty-five, he's reaching that point where the lines are converging precipitously.

Louis has brought drinks for his mother and for him-

self, and a fresh one for me. I thank him, and we talk about
the New York mayoral campaign in which he has been involved. He has funny stories, of course, of vanity and in-
competence and petty jealousies. They'd be ugly stories, I
suppose, if a mean sort of person told them. But Louis is a
good kid.

People are making toasts, mostly to Abe, but some to
Bob and Greta, who are, after all, our hosts. Someone pro-
poses "Those who are not here," which is well intended perhaps, but gauche. The room sobers. We think of Aunt
Jenny, Abe's late wife, who isn't here. And my father, who
was younger than Abe. And my mother. And Uncle Carl.
And Susie, down in Washington . . . The conversation re-
sumes with an almost willful liveliness.

People are starting to drift toward the tables. I keep
close to Louis and Aunt Tady, not only because I hardly
know any of the others but because it is not likely that there
will be many more occasions to have a meal with the two
of them. And Bob and Greta join us, so our table is altogether familiar—in both senses. It is my reward, I suppose,
for being a good boy.

But I'm wrong. My reward is a piece of information,
and I cannot remember how we got onto the subject. We
must have been talking about names, one way or another,
and toward the end of the meal I ask Aunt Tady what her
name is. I mean, her real name. Tady, after all, isn't a
name. I was so young a child when I first heard it that it
never crossed my mind that it was unusual in any way. So
many names and words were unknown to me that I generally assumed my ignorance was enough to account for any
unfamiliarity. But time has passed, and now I am willing to
risk the rudeness of putting a direct question, particularly
about a name, to an aunt who has been as close to me, I
suppose, as any relative outside what social scientists would
call our nuclear unit.

She stares at me, and I can't tell if it is an angry glare or a more baleful look of someone who feels attacked and is hurt.

"It must be short for something," I say, "or based on something. I've never even heard of another Tady." I am smiling and trying to seem friendly.

"Well, if you must know," she says, "it's short for Tatiana, which in Russia—"

"—was wonderful!" I interrupt. "What a great name! I love that name! One of the grand duchesses was Tatiana, and there's a Tatiana in *Eugene Onegin*."

"Yes," she tells me, beaming, "but not many people in Bridgeport knew that. It wasn't an easy name . . ." And she smiles now so that I can glimpse what she must have looked like thirty years ago. She is relieved that I'm not attacking her or making fun of her, and pleased that I like her name.

"Tatiana," I say once again. "Yes, it would have been difficult, but they were wrong."

She closes her eyes to what is a piece of nonsense. And the moment passes. Then there is a cake for Uncle Abe and more toasts, and here and there people are dabbing at their eyes. We all sing "Happy Birthday," and then the waiters and waitresses bring around coffeepots and brandy bottles.

Somebody says we must get together in five years and do this again, and my cousin Bob promises, "You're on!"

Half an hour later, I'm on the road, heading south, and thinking about the party. I ask myself the obvious questions, wondering what the point was, what was accomplished. Is there any real bond between an uncle and a nephew? Or between cousins? The connection is theoretical, or emblematic. We have matching crocheted afghans our grandmother made for both of us before she died.

Still, for my father's sake, I guess I'm glad I went.

I am on the Connecticut Turnpike, which is where my uncle's money comes from. He was one of the big players in the condemnation game, back when they were taking the land for that road in the late forties. Every fifty- or hundred- or two-hundred-foot piece of it was a separate case, and most of these cases went to court, and my uncle got a percentage of whatever he could win in the courts over and above the original offer from the State of Connecticut. Not a very complicated or intellectually fascinating area of the law—as my father often observed—but lucrative. And as I drive, the flashing of the broken lane lines suggests entries in my uncle's bank account back in the days of his prime.

A bonanza. A Comstock lode! Hooray for Abe!

Of course, this swath of road is rich in other ways, too. The events of my life could be located and identified by historical markers like the one I'm passing for Israel Putnam's cottage. Even without the markers, I find myself reacting to the various exits with pleasure or pain or regret or some subtler combination of feelings. It was this exit we took to the kennel where we bought a cocker spaniel when I was nine. And this was the exit we took to the Clam Box, where my mother and father liked to take us out to dinner for birthdays. And farther down is the exit to the cemetery where they are buried.

The last time I was on this road was only a couple of weeks ago, when I drove up with my sister to visit her younger daughter, who'd just started at college. And it was at this part of the road that we found the klezmer music on WEVD. It was funny, schmaltzy, ridiculous music to which we responded with both laughter and sadness, laughter for its excesses and its naïveté, and sadness for what we miss, what has leached out of our lives. One of the pieces was a version of "Rozhinkes mit Mandlen," or "Raisins and Almonds," which my mother used to sing to me when I was very young. I remember that. I didn't know whether my sister remembered it or not. And, not knowing the answer, I was reluctant to ask her.

She noticed that I was rubbing my eyes, which I had to do in order to see so I could drive. She didn't say anything. And I didn't say anything. But later on, when we were in my niece's dormitory room and I was flipping idly through the course catalog, I noticed that a prominent Israeli poet was on the campus for the year as a visiting professor and that he was teaching a course in medieval Hebrew poetry.

I suggested to my niece that she might ask if the course was in English and, if so, request permission to audit.

I mean, why not? One of my old teachers used to tell me that it wasn't terribly important what the subject was, but that I should always study with great men if there were any around. They were the real subjects of their courses. And it's true and useful and something I've told my own children.

But my niece wasn't having any of that. "I'm afraid I'm disinterested in medieval Hebrew poetry," she said.

"You mean *un*interested," I corrected.

"Oh, come on!" she protested. "I don't need grammar lessons from you."

"Why not from me? You need them from someone," I said. "And it's better to hear these things from family than from strangers, isn't it?"

"No," she said, "it isn't."

"Okay," I said, and shut up.

Thinking of that, I consider what it is to be an uncle, or a niece or nephew. If an uncle can be hurt, as I was, then an uncle may also be pleased—as I hope Abe was.

I do not understand the words to "Rozhinkes mit Mandlen." If I were to go back to school now, to take courses rather than give them, I'd study only languages. And Yiddish and Hebrew would be among them.

My niece is only a freshman and will grow out of it. She will learn the difference between *disinterested* and *uninterested* and also perhaps acquire a little tact and sense.

And maybe, over time, even the beginnings of wisdom. But if there are tunes that bring tears to her eyes, they will not be any my sister or I recognize. Or that our parents or grandparents would have known. My nieces and my own children will not be able to understand *Beh-meh*. And they will not even have an afghan to hold on to.

And if, in the dimness or blaze of light of old age, some confused relative takes one of them for his or her parent, will he or she consent out of politeness? And how will it feel to be my sister for a few minutes, or to be me? Will they do a worse job of it than I did this evening?

It is a dumb thing to worry about. Driving down his road to watch his son's horses running at Aqueduct or at Belmont, my uncle Abe doesn't worry about such things.

Or maybe he does.

Name Six Famous Belgians

What they give you when you check into the Villa Igiea is a little card to carry with you—but not in your wallet, presumably—to certify that you are a guest in the hotel and that you are insured. The pamphlet that comes with the card explains the insurance policy the hotel carries that covers you in case your pocket is picked, your wallet stolen, your purse snatched, or even worse. If you have a mind to, you can read through the impressive document until you get to the clause about how, if you are hospitalized, your next of kin will be brought to Palermo from anywhere in the world. Or about how, if you are killed, your body will be shipped home at no charge to your estate.

Bad as it is back in Philadelphia, it has not yet come to this. But then Palermo has had a couple of millennia headstart.

With a straight face, Harry thanked the desk clerk, but when they got up to their room, he and Joan made nervous jokes about it. Out through the double doors of their balcony they could see the glassy Mediterranean, more pacific than the Pacific. They simply couldn't believe it—not that there could be such lawlessness as the insurance company's document implied, but that it could be so taken for granted. Harry supposed it was remotely possible that this could be a gesture the management made to give the tourists a pleasant frisson of fear, to suggest without seriously inconveniencing anyone the depredations either of the

Mafia or merely of the desperately poor. It would be going too far to subject their guests to the disagreeable business of an actual mugging.

Far from the center of town, the Villa Igiea is secluded in its own gardened enclave. From the balcony of their room, Harry and Joan could look left to the open sea. A little to the right, they could see a couple of giant cranes of the port. The city itself, though, was out of sight, even farther to the right and behind them. Harry's idea had been that a certain degree of insulation from the abrasions of life in a strange and poor city would be a good thing, especially on the first days of their visit when they were still acclimating themselves not only to local customs but also to the water and the time of day. Recovering from jet lag, they wanted at least the possibility of respite from assaults by Sicilian exuberance.

And it looked as though it would work out just as they'd hoped. The only trouble was that, being a little way out of town, they had to drive to do any sight-seeing or to eat anywhere except in the hotel dining room, and the map Avis had given them was almost useless. It did not show one-way streets, which was essential in a place like Palermo. Navigation was further complicated by the absence of any systematic posting of street signs. It was one thing to find a street on a map, but quite another to find it out in the real world. This was Joan's job, and she complained a lot. Harry complained, too, about the stick shift of the underpowered and overgeared Fiat Uno they'd been given and the erratic driving habits of the Sicilians, who slowed down for red lights but did not feel obliged to come to anything as deferential as a full stop. And people on motor scooters wove through the traffic in a demonstration of a death wish, the fulfillment of which was occasionally celebrated by a blare of sirens from ambulances and police cars, which in their haste contributed to the excitement and general sense of peril.

44

It was in an attempt to circumvent the busy center of town and save themselves a little time and stress that they got lost on the morning of their second day. And perhaps they were a little crabby with each other, too. Joan kept insisting that Harry pull over and stop so that she could find where they were on the wretched Avis map. Eventually he did so, but gracelessly. He stared through the windshield, making no effort to hide his impatience with her. Hers was an easier job, after all, and if he could do the driving, then she ought to be able to keep track of where they were and where they wanted to go. He waited while she pored over the tiny print of the map on her lap, and then quite suddenly she screamed. Harry turned toward her, not yet thinking anything, but shocked, this being an excessive display of her frustration with the map and with him. He was startled and puzzled, and not quite certain that he'd seen what he thought he'd seen—the blur of a disappearing hand.

"He tried to grab my purse," Joan said. Her voice was high, not shrill but unnaturally thin.

Harry's head turned further. Through the back window, he could see—no question now—the would-be purse snatcher, straddling a bicycle perhaps six feet behind the car, and ready to flee if they should try to pursue him. He might have been thirteen or so. He looked even younger, maybe eleven, but then Sicilians are small, and the diet of the poorest of them must be very meager indeed.

"Drive!" Joan commanded through clenched teeth, her voice still strained. "Let's get out of here."

He drove. They rolled the windows up until they were almost closed and checked the door locks. They kept going until they found an unfrightening part of town and a place where they could park and go into a bar for a coffee. It had been an invasion, of course, a terrible intrusion, and what had kept the boy from getting the purse was the seatbelt that had covered the shoulder strap of Joan's purse, securing it. They'd left their passports and most of their traveler's checks back at the hotel. And for the first time they had been wearing their moneybelts, light navy-blue nylon articles that they had strapped on that morning after breakfast, feeling a little silly. And, Harry reminded Joan, there was that insurance policy the hotel carried!

She laughed, a single sardonic snort. No harm had been done. Still, the idea of the thing was nasty, the disesteem it implied that one human being should have for another. That the thief had been only a child made it worse, if anything. Youngsters are supposed to be innocent and only later to fall from grace as they are called by the necessities of survival to compromise their original principles of fairness and decency. (This was the fiction to which they pretended to subscribe most of the time, if only because the alternative was so uncomfortable: what kind of a world would it be in which such risks and violences are normal?)

The carping about the driving and the map reading stopped, now that something more serious had intruded upon them. With a studied determination—so as not to admit to themselves or each other that they had been defeated or even much affected by this small, nasty incident—they pushed on with their search for the road to Monreale, found it, made their pilgrimage, and even managed to enjoy the extraordinary cathedral with its dazzling mosaics and the cloister next door with that wonderfully various colonnade.

By that evening the incident had been all but forgotten. Neither of them at any rate made mention of it. It is possible, of course, that one or the other of them might have found this omission just a bit peculiar, might have wondered at the other's diffidence, but for her part she might have been reluctant to probe at what was perhaps a tender place. And he might have attributed to her silence a solicitude that was at once welcome and intolerable—because he hated to be condescended to or treated as other than healthy and sane. The closest they'd come to that kind of therapeutic attention had been her asking him, back home in the dark, when neither had to look at the other's facial expression or body language, if he was sure he wanted to go to Italy.

"It's Magna Graecia we're going to see," he had said, "Greek ruins and a few Norman churches and some Bourbon buildings."

"I know," she had said, "but still . . ."

"It's okay," he'd told her.

How far beyond that could she have pushed?

And here he was, and even after what had happened, he seemed to be okay.

For the next few days, it was still okay. He was, or it was. Nobody else in Palermo tried to rob them or mug them or kill them. And they drove out, heading east toward Cefalù, with memories of good food and fine buildings and some memorable statuary in the archaeological museum. And most of the good stuff was still to come: Taormina, the mosaics in the remains of the Imperial Villa at Piazza Armerina, and the avenue of temples in Agrigento. And their mood was okay—good enough at least so that at the worst each was, for the sake of the other, putting up a good front. But as each of them knew, to be able still to do that is to be in reasonable shape.

They both had the feeling that they deserved a good time. For one thing they hadn't taken a vacation in almost two years. For another, they'd spent all those evenings planning this trip, working out the sights they wanted to see, and the distances, and the hotels where it would be fun to stay. One of the high points was going to be Agrigento, which was perhaps grounds for a certain skepticism. To have excessive expectations is to be vulnerable to disappointment. Still, there was a picture of the Temple of Concord on the cover of their *Blue Guide* showing between the inner and outer colonnades a narrow swath of sky, and one

47

could see the rough texture of the caramel-colored marble stucco of the columns, which had been baking in the Sicilian sun for a couple of millennia. That the editors had put this on the cover meant it had to be good, didn't it? That was an accolade even greater than its three stars in the text and its bold print in the index.

They were wary, but it was impossible for them never to let their hopes off the leash. And as it turned out, they were astonished, absolutely delighted when the Villa Athena porter, having shown them to their room, drew back the curtains, opened the shutters of the French windows that gave onto their patio, and stood back to reveal, just outside and up a little rise, the avenue of the temples. Directly in front of them was the Temple of Concord, in such a remarkable state of preservation that it looked theatrical. It was odd, certainly, so that Harry laughed, not at the temple or even at himself and his wariness, but just because a thing like that could be in the world, could be real, let alone so close. It was like an exotic bird that had lit on a branch right outside their window, an unlooked-for grace. Joan reacted in much the same way but didn't laugh, because she didn't want to scare it away.

There was no point in going anywhere or doing anything. They didn't have to discuss it. They decided just to stay where they were, drink things from the Frigo-bar, and look at the temple. Later they'd go out, climb up to it, and walk around it, but that could keep a while, until the cool of the afternoon. For now, it was more than enough that they could just stare at it, try to grasp it, try to let it soak in. Joan put on her bathing suit and went out to the terrace with a book so that she could sun herself, reading a sentence or two but then looking up every now and again for another confirmation that, yes, it was still there, presiding over its quarter of the sky. Inside, Harry lay down on the bed and watched television, not because he was interested in dubbed

American soap operas but for the contrast between the familiarly tacky program and what was there outside the room, unfamiliar and untacky, and available to him without his even having to turn his head. All he had to do was adjust his eyeballs ever so slightly and there it was, not a figment of his imagination, but real, actual, substantial. The program changed to something called "Dada-Oompah," just as dumb but Italian. The building did not go away.

"Okay?" he called out.

"Terrific!" she answered. And then, after a beat, she ventured to ask, "Happy?"

"Oh, yeah!"

The terrace, it turned out, was not theirs alone but was shared with the room across the hall, which was why there was a row of planters down the middle. Late that afternoon, Harry and Joan walked over to inspect the Temple of Herakles, the Temple of Hera, the Temple of Zeus, and their own—they actually thought of it that way now—Temple of Concord. When they got back to their room, they found that their neighbors had established themselves on the terrace, as of course it was their right to do. They were a slightly younger couple, in their early forties maybe, English as it turned out. He was an investment banker. She was in publishing. She was Dotty. He was Paul.

It wasn't as bad as it might have been. In fact, there was a kind of advantage to small talk with the English couple much like the benefit of having the television set turned on. One could talk about ordinary things, exchange trivial information—that *nespolle,* for instance, those unimpressive little fruits they had been seeing on restaurant dessert carts, were the medlars Giovanni Verga mentioned in his title, or that Luigi Pirandello had been born down there, between the new city and the sea. And then one could glance again at the ridge and see the Temple of Concord, still there, still gorgeous, or perhaps even slightly more gorgeous, those earth-brown tones having deepened now as the sun sank toward the horizon.

The two couples sat there on either side of their planter-divider, drinking Campari and soda from their Frigo-bars and keeping watch on the temple. Paul said that the great event at the hotel was sitting in the outdoor dining pavilion and watching the temple disappear into the darkness and then reemerge abruptly when they turned the arc lights on. It was a good idea to plan to eat around eight in order to catch this. Harry thanked him. There was a delicate moment in which each considered making the suggestion that the four of them dine together, but nobody said anything. Perhaps each had been waiting for one of the others to make the overture that never came. At any rate, the moment passed. They finished their drinks and wished one another a good evening.

But when Harry and Joan went down to dinner, they saw that almost all the tables were occupied. A bus had deposited a crowd of tourists, Germans mostly, who weren't staying at the hotel but were eating there, perhaps for that dramatic moment of the illumination Paul had talked about. Harry and Joan had already resigned themselves to waiting, but the head waiter came back to ask if they would like to share the far table with the couple there who had suggested that they join them. They looked to see Paul and Dotty waving encouragingly.

"Shall we?" Harry asked.

"We can't not," Joan said.

They followed the head waiter to Paul and Dotty's table, thanked them, and sat down. The English couple had arrived just a few moments earlier and had not yet ordered. Harry suggested champagne as the only appropriate way to toast that temple off to the south. Or the closest local equivalent, which was Asti Spumanti.

It was a pleasant dinner, and, yes, there was a moment

when the lights switched on and the temple, a dimmed shape, sprang back into a sudden and almost garish clarity. After their meal, they went into the bar for coffee and exchanged itineraries and stories. At one point, Paul mentioned an odd custom Dotty had heard of when she'd gone to the Frankfurt Book Fair. Some of the London publishers take the ferry across to Ostend and then drive to Frankfurt because it's cheaper that way, he said. And as they make their way through Belgium, the game is to name six famous Belgians before they get to the German border. "And the wonderful thing," he said, "is that it can't be done."

"Can't it?" Harry asked, though not combatively. "Leopold and Beaudoin, for starters. And Paul-Henri Spaak."

"Yes, but then it gets tough," Paul said, grinning.

"I guess it does. Glière, maybe. His people were Belgian, anyway."

"Doubtful, but okay."

"Hercule Poirot?" Joan asked.

"He's fictional. He doesn't count, I'm afraid," Dotty said, shaking her head. "People always try him when they get desperate enough."

"Okay, okay," Joan agreed.

"Maybe that's a good thing, though," Harry said. "I mean, that it's so tough. I like the idea of ordinary people leading ordinary lives."

"And eating good food. The food in Brussels is wonderful," Paul said.

"Famous people," Harry said, "are frequently villains."

There was a moment, but the conversation resumed, and there were suggestions about their all getting together again one day, in New York, maybe, or in London. They actually exchanged addresses before they went up to their hallway to separate and retire for the night.

"Nice people," Joan said, once the door was closed.

"Yes, they were," Harry said.

"Well, they still are, aren't they?"

"I suppose so, yes," he admitted. And then, as an afterthought, "Funny about the Belgians. I can't think of any more."

"Neither can I."

They did get swindled once. They discovered it only when they were back in Palermo waiting for the ferry to take them up to Naples. They went into a little place on the Via Cavour for iced coffee, and at the cashier's desk, Harry peeled off what he thought was the right amount of Italian money, only to be told that one of the bills he'd offered, a five-hundred-lire note, was no good. These had been recalled more than a year ago. There was a coin now for that denomination—which was worth at the time maybe thirty-three cents. Harry shook his head, realizing that he'd been taken, that only tourists would be ignorant enough to be victimized this way, and put the worthless note back into his wallet. But he didn't seem really upset. Joan observed all this and was encouraged. And she began to relax, now that Sicily was mostly behind them.

They took the Tirrenia, which got them to Naples at six in the morning. Their plans were to spend a few days in Naples, going down to Pompeii and Herculaneum, and then to take a *rapido* up to Rome to do some shopping and be entertained by some of Harry's old friends. The trip, Joan thought, had gone well enough. They'd not only not had a bad time, but they'd enjoyed an affirmatively good one. And when they got to Naples, Harry again seemed no more than wryly amused by the petty thievery of the cab driver who had charged so exorbitantly for a ride of only a few blocks from the dock to their hotel on the Via Partenope, claiming surcharges because it was Sunday morning, because it was not yet seven so the night rates were still in effect, and because they had baggage and he'd been obliged to open the trunk. Harry groused that he'd thought he was hiring the entire cab, trunk included, but he paid and he even smiled.

So Joan thought she could relax. She took only the precautions any prudent American tourist tries to remember to take, always walking so that Harry was on the street side and taking care that her bag was clutched tightly under her arm. And in Naples they never came any closer to getting robbed than they had on that second day in Palermo. Their net loss to crime on the whole trip was that thirty-three cents, the value of that recalled note.

The assault—if it was an assault—came from a different and altogether unexpected quarter, from the soccer madness that gripped the nation and especially caught up the Neapolitans. The World Cup matches were going on in Mexico, and all over Naples there were Italian flags hanging out of apartment windows, the official red-white-and-green tricolor or homemade banners with "Forza Italia" lettered in those colors. Sometimes they stretched across streets from one building to another, on lines that were ordinarily used to hang laundry.

Harry and Joan went out to dinner one night at a little pizzeria they'd found a few blocks from the hotel. It had looked lively enough when they'd first spotted it, crowded and inviting, but this evening it was almost deserted. And the waiter spent most of his time in the back room, watching the Italian team struggle with the South Koreans in an effort not to get eliminated. Evidently, all of Naples was engaged in this effort half a world away, for whenever the Italian team did something good, there would be an encouraging blast of automobile horns from the cars outside. It was all right if they wanted to enjoy themselves that way, but the waiter's inattention was irksome. Harry had to get up and find him to ask for the bill.

"Didn't you want coffee?" Joan asked.

"Yes, but not there. Let's go someplace else. Someplace nice—where they care about the customers. This is nuts."

"It's sports. You like sports."

"This is worse than that. It's nationalism. It's madness. What the hell difference will it make to anybody in Naples if the Italian team beats the South Koreans?"

"It takes their minds off their troubles," she suggested, not wanting to argue.

"What minds? It lets them reveal their true character. That's what it really does. And that's ugly."

Joan could have answered him in a number of ways. He'd been the one who had insisted on Italy, for God's sake! And she'd once asked him, point-blank, "Are you sure you want to do this?" But he'd looked at her and nodded, as if to say that he wasn't going to be deprived of Italy, too.

As if to say that it was not significant that the thug who had broken into his mother's house to burglarize it, whom his mother had confronted, and who had bludgeoned her to death happened to be Italian. Two years later, Harry had been talking about Italy, about Sicily in particular, and how he'd never been there. It made perfect sense, but Joan was shrewd enough to distrust sense. She'd seen Harry piece himself back together, a crude patching job like that of a child mending a sugar bowl he had dropped, gluing the shards together as well as he could.

She'd asked him that, but only once. Because when he reacted, it was unpredictable whether he would lash out or just collapse inwardly. And in neither event was it good to be close by.

They walked from the pizzeria back past their hotel and on toward the Piazza del Martiri, the district of chic shops where they had noticed a flossy coffee bar and gelateria with outside tables. There were plenty of empty tables now, and there were a couple of waiters standing ready to bring ice cream or coffee. They weren't inside, huddled around some television set. Harry seemed satisfied, and he and Joan sat down and ordered—coffee ice cream for her and *zuppa inglese* ice cream for him. The waiter brought their order right away.

And then, in Mexico City, the Italians came from behind to beat the South Koreans, and in Naples, everybody went wild. They bolted from their apartments, jumped into their cars or onto their motorcycles or scooters, unfurled their enormous flags and banners, and raced through the streets yelling and blowing their horns. The street, which had been quiet a moment before, was alive with people now, swarming with traffic, loud, blaring, grating, triumphant, frenzied, insisting on the wonderfulness of their being Italians, their national pride and ebullience bubbling up and spewing forth.

She watched Harry retreating into himself, watched his color drain, the muscles along his jaw twitch, the tears well up in his eyes and spill down his cheeks. What they were insisting upon was exactly what he could not bear, what he hated: the barbarousness that was the verso of their culture, their potentiality for cruelty and violence, the thuggish nastiness they could assume when they assembled into crowds for a Mussolini to harangue, passionate oafs ready to be seduced by villains and clowns.

"You want to go?" she asked.

He couldn't speak. He only nodded.

He threw a few thousand lire onto the table. He hesitated. Then he threw that worthless five-hundred-lire note onto the pile with it.

They started back toward the hotel, a matter of five blocks or so, but they were a long five blocks, and there were wide streets to cross, dangerous in the Mezzogiorno at the best of times and utterly intimidating now. There was a couple on a Vespa, a young man with a young woman behind him, and they had a dog running along beside them on a leash, and the dog was struggling to keep up. Joan saw it and saw that Harry saw it, noting his grimace of pain and rage . . . and she could do nothing.

Back at the hotel, their bed had been turned down. The shutters were closed and the heavy draperies pulled closed, but they could still hear the blare of horns, that mindless mechanical braying as tireless as it was inescapable. The best they could do was to undress and go to bed. Harry took a long pull of brandy from the bottle they carried with them, got into bed, and put his head under a pillow that could not possibly have blocked out the noise but maybe muffled it a little.

Joan turned on the television set, found a channel that was broadcasting something other than the gloating interviews about the soccer victory—an old "Mission Impossible" episode, actually—and turned up the volume. There was no response from Harry, but at least he didn't object. Eventually, she supposed, he'd fall asleep. And eventually he did.

In the morning they were subdued, like people with hangovers, but they did what they'd planned to do. They went over to Capri for the day, didn't like it, came back, packed, and took the train to Rome early the next morning.

Rome was all right. "River City," one of their American friends who lived there called it. They were there for three days, during which Joan kept looking surreptitiously at her watch, counting the hours until they could make their way through Da Vinci's impressive array of guards and inspectors and board the plane heading home.

For those first few weeks after their return, friends in Philadelphia asked them about their vacation and where they'd gone. The first time it happened, Harry surprised Joan, lying blandly and outrageously. "Belgium," he said, absolutely straight-faced.

56

"Oh? And how was it?" they asked, politely.

Harry let Joan tell them. It was, at last, something she could do, something he could let her do for him.

"Wonderful," she said. "Very peaceful. A wonderful country."

"The whole time? In Belgium?"

"Oh, yes," Harry said, glancing at her in a quick look of acknowledgment that was like an embrace. "It's a fine place. The food in Brussels is wonderful."

The Long Island Train

My father used to tell a story. He said it was
true, and that he'd heard it from somebody who
used to translate advertisements from national
campaigns into Yiddish so they could run in the
Jewish *Daily Forward*. And that felt right because
there was a Talmudic quality to this, as there was
to many of his favorite stories. I often think of my
father as misplaced here, out of his element. He'd
have been more at home as a rabbi with a small
court in Russia or Poland. Not that my grandparents were wrong to come here. Oh, no! No question but that it was the smartest thing anyone in
the family has done in the last hundred years.
Still, against every gain there are losses to be tal-
lied, costs to be paid.

My father's story is about a woman who has
been told how to go to the Bronx on the old Third
Avenue El. Back in those days, there used to be a
junction at Fifty-seventh Street, or maybe it was
Fifty-ninth. But in there somewhere the tracks
would diverge, one branch going north to the
Bronx and the other swinging east to Long Island.
The woman on the platform has been told to take
any train except the one that was going to Long
Island, which is a fairly simple thing. And with
this in mind, she asks a gentleman on the platform
which is the Long Island train. He tells her that
the Long Island train has one green light and one
amber light on the front and that all the other trains
go to the Bronx. She thanks him. The next train
that comes in has two amber lights on the front,

and when the doors open, she starts to enter the first car. The man comes chasing after her to stop her, saying, "No, no, lady, this isn't the one you want. This isn't the Long Island train!" She gives him a look, and as the doors close, she asks, "So who wants the Long Island train?"

And that's it. Except that it isn't. The story reverberates, rolls on through time, has lasted longer than the steel girders of the old el and rattles still in my head. It's surprising how often it turns out to be relevant, that we have misconstrued what people's real intentions were, leapt to conclusions that seemed obvious but that were altogether wrong.

It is also alive in a specific and geographical way. I cannot drive across Westchester on Route 287 without seeing the exits for White Plains or pass those exit signs without asking aloud, "So who wants the Long Island train?"

The White Plains I knew is as completely gone as the Third Avenue El. I can remember when it started to go, the day Macy's opened its branch store at the corner of Main Street and Mamaroneck Avenue and the small town I just barely remember got its first escalator, which seemed to me a glamorous big-city device. The final collapse, though, was in 1948, when Temple Israel moved from Fisher Avenue out to Old Mamaroneck Road and changed its name to the Temple Israel Community Center, a typically Byzantine thing to do, affirming the value—community—only to mark its death.

The old temple is a black church now, which was probably predictable. That part of town had gone somewhat to seed. The prosperous congregation had moved away. Why not build a new building in a better area, and as long as they were at it, why not throw in a gymnasium and a wing for the Hebrew school? It all made perfect sense. Who can blame them?

59

I can, of course. The old temple had wooden benches. There was a severe formality about that which still seems right. One ought not make oneself too comfortable in God's house, after all. The new Community Center has in its sanctuary seats that were designed for movie theaters, all upholstered and comfy. For the tender *tuchises* of the all-rightnicks who were contributing to the new edifice.

I think mine was the last bar mitzvah in the old building, which is how I date the move. I can still vividly remember being let out of Hebrew school on Fisher Avenue early one afternoon because news had broken about the death of President Roosevelt. I remember trudging up the long Lexington Avenue hill, worrying about the country and, more specifically, about my parents and whether they would cry. Which frightened me a little. I hadn't yet lived through a death in the family, didn't know what to do on such occasions, and was worried that I'd do or say the wrong thing. And I was frightened because if the president could die, then my parents could die. Anyone could die. I could die myself.

It is a scary thing to confront when you're nine.

But when you have confronted it, well or badly, the place where that happened is marked, is holy. I cannot imagine that in the old country they moved to better parts of town and built new synagogues. Not often, anyway.

That Fisher Avenue temple, then, is a lost world, my equivalent of the old country, a modest shtetl-like community. The faces of the boys who were in classes with me, some of them friends and some not, are all vivid in my mind and curiously important, as though they were *landsmen*. And the faces and the figures, too, of the girls, giggling and secretive, who were at that age so much more grown up . . .

A black church now, the building still stands, but nothing is left there to visit or show to one's children or grandchildren. It is as lost as those villages with names like sneezes that my grandparents remembered, or tried to remember and couldn't.

That a large area surrounding a Galleria still calls itself White Plains is a coincidence, a crude joke. Like Poles or Cossacks or Huns or Nazis, prosperity and urban renewal have done away with anything I recognize. Even after their sacrifices and heroic exertions, I am no more at home there or anywhere than my parents were, or my grandparents, which is sad. Where I feel at home is in my head, where I carry around tag lines I remember from my father's jokes.

I was driving around not long ago with my daughter-in-law in Somerville, Massachusetts, and we passed a store on Mass Avenue where I had shopped once but that had gone out of business. "I wonder why?" I asked without thinking. The same dumb question I'd asked my father when I was a kid. My daughter-in-law answered instantly and automatically. "They were making too much money."

My father's line. She'd never even heard him say it. She'd picked it up from my son. And their son will say it, too, whether he knows where it came from or not. It is where we live. It is where rabbis and writers have to live because buildings keep getting torn down, along with elevated railway lines and cities and whole countries.

Another story my father used to tell was about an aunt of his who spoke no English at all, but who knew how to visit her sister—in Long Island, as a matter of fact. She got on a certain train with lights disposed a certain way, rode for a certain number of stops, got out, walked a few blocks, made a turn at the corset maker's shop, walked one more block, and there was her sister's building. But one day she got lost, wandered around aimlessly all day, and only by great luck and the kindness of strangers managed to get home again. The damned corset maker had closed up. Out of business, maybe. (Making too much money?) Or dead. But my father's aunt couldn't understand that and kept asking, "How could he do such a thing to people who were depending on him?"

Grandfather

There they were, the two stuffed animals, cheek by jowl on the white changing table my son had put together in the room he'd turned into a nursery. I was up in Boston on business, but also to visit Ben and Ruth. Ruth was a month away from delivering my first grandchild. And on that changing table Ben had set out the two toys. I recognized mine—an absurdly expensive but irresistible English bulldog in soft plush with a soulful expression on its wrinkled face. It had huge feet and, elegantly executed, the rose ears of real bulldogs. The other, I knew right away, was Irene's. No question! It was a white baby seal with a little pamphlet around its neck explaining all about gray seals and their terrible plight. There was also a Wildlife Federation button that the child could wear as soon as it became old enough to turn itself into a bulletin board for righteous causes.

I'm being sarcastic, but why not? The idea of fairness is just one of life's ways of lulling you out of your natural alertness.

I looked at those two plush toys and thought: Oh, boy (or girl)! You aren't even born yet, aren't due for a month, and already you're in big trouble. How are you going to negotiate through this minefield of plush toys and not-so-plush intentions?

Irene and I have been divorced for years now. Divorce is supposed to get better after a while, but I'm still waiting. (It is flattering, I guess, that she still cares enough to be so bitchy, but there it is.) It wasn't just Irene that was getting me down, though. It was Boston, too.

Boston was never a lucky town for me. I am not especially superstitious, but I learned long ago, when I was a kid younger than Ben and starting out in New York, that there were lucky buildings and there were others that were forbidding in their auguries and omens—places where I could tell just by the feel of their lobbies that I'd never make a dime from any of the firms on their directories. It's true with cities, too. Having been away for some years, I was impressed by how nice the new subways looked in Boston, but even so, I kept looking for some wraith of my old self, skulking about on one of the platforms, on the way to a job interview perhaps or, more vividly, to an afternoon tryst.

Mostly, though, I thought of Ben and Ruth's wedding and what a miracle it was that I managed to drive away, negotiating the Mass Pike without getting killed, being unable to see much more than blurred hints of the road through the tears that kept welling up. They were tears of shame and anger—and of self-pity, too, I am bold to admit. But then, those are the hottest, bitterest kind.

Not that I wallow still in those old emotions. I have put most of that behind me. Still, when the baby is born, I shall have to come back here and deal with it all again, confront Irene, and continue the old struggles. Yes, I know, it's supposed to be a fresh start and a clean slate that the kid starts out with, but as Henry Adams told us long ago, there are no such things.

I sometimes think I ought to have stayed away from the wedding. The only thing worse than being beaten is not admitting it and trying to carry on, keeping a stiff upper lip. On the other hand, I couldn't have stayed away. Two years before, when I'd remarried, I'd asked Ben to come out to California to be my best man. I hadn't twisted his arm. I had set it up so that he could decline if he felt really uncomfortable about it. But then, he's not stupid, and he knew how much it meant to me to have him there, for himself, of course, but also representing his brother and sister and their assent if not their positive approval. Whether he meant it or not when he said he'd be happy to, he actually did haul his ass over to Logan, and he flew out to be there with me when I married Joan.

It cost him. And I don't mean the plane fare. I saw the carbon copy of the letter Irene sent him—the copy was the whole point, actually; she had sent him the original only so she could send me that carbon. Rage, venom, wild accusations that Ben had betrayed her, and elaborate theatrical curses. She'd obviously spent a long time composing this screed, delighting in it before loosing it upon us. I read it and my heart sank, and I called Ben to tell him again that he didn't have to come. But he said she'd get over it and, anyway, he'd promised. He would be there. And he was.

So I owed him. And two years later, when he and Ruth were getting married, I had to be there. Even if Irene had set it up so that Joan was not invited. It wasn't even Irene's party, for God's sake! Ruth's mother was the hostess, at least in theory. But Irene issued one of her ultimata, announcing that she'd come only on condition that Joan didn't. She was going to be there with Albert. (Were they married by then? I don't think so.) But that didn't matter. I was told I had to leave Joan home.

Unfair, of course, not only to me but to Ben. It was a cheap way of using Ben as a weapon with which to bludgeon me. And me as a weapon with which to get back at him. She could make us both pay. All Ben wanted was for both of his parents to be there, and the only way that could be worked was for him to present Irene's preposterous condition to me and for me to accede to it.

I could have agreed and then pretended to be sick. Or claimed to have had car trouble. I'd have been able to figure out some plausible excuse. But if I hadn't gone, then my mother would have had no way to get there. So I was caught between my own inclination to preserve my dignity and my obligations both to my son and my mother.

The family style—my late father's style, that is—made it even tougher. In our house, affronts were not easily forgiven. Slights were remembered for years, even decades. My father banished people, as if he were some Eastern monarch of unlimited powers—which is crazy, but this was how he behaved, and how I thought it was right for me to behave, too.

Irene knew this, of course. One of the lovely things about divorce is that the parties know each other, have learned the tender places that are sore from old wounds and vulnerable to new proddings. Irene knew how stiff-necked I could be, how stiff-necked I thought it was right to be. She had been there, for instance, when my father had his first operation and we went to see him, concerned about him, worried about whether he'd make it through surgery. And he'd been furious because I had grown a beard. "Like the schwartzer orderly!" he said. "He's got a beard just like that."

Of course, that wasn't what bothered him. Beards were for rabbis or, to make it even clearer, for immigrants. A clean-shaven face is assimilated and enlightened. Beards are either for greenhorns or for bums, for raffish bohemians who do not take seriously the striving and the self-denials of people like my father. Painters, writers, jazz musicians, all the creatures of sensation whom the schwartzer orderly admired and whom my father feared, they wore beards. I was coming to see him because I cared about him, but what he saw was an agent from the enemy camp, a foreigner or a stranger, but either way an affront to his whole life. And his father's as well. The entire family history had been this project of which I was supposed to be the ornament, and I was ignoring it, throwing away what he had worked so hard to hand to me, for no reason at all or, worse, for a bad reason—stupid vanity and heedless modishness.

It is unremarkable, a sad but banal story, except that from his hospital bed he issued an ultimatum: I was not to return to the hospital until I'd shaved the damned beard off my face.

"What? You're kidding!" I protested.

"I'm not kidding at all," he'd said, his voice subdued, which could be even more menacing than the thundering yell. Subdued, but by no means soft. Oh, no, it was hard and icy, the way men can be when their lives are at stake.

I got the message. I knew that if I didn't shave the damned beard, and if he died, I'd never forgive myself. Or that it was even worse and more intricate—that if I didn't shave the beard, my stubbornness would in some mysterious way bring about my father's death, the long shot paying off only because an idiot had been rash enough to bet on it.

And my father knew exactly what I'd be thinking, how I'd rage at the unfairness of it, and how eventually I'd clip the beard down to a length where a safety razor could deal with it and then lather up—the way I'd learned to do, watching him in the bathroom—and shave it off.

As, of course, I did. And I've gone clean-shaven ever since.

Ben has a beard, though. To which my father never objected. Not that he approved of it, but he was a realist and knew he'd lose if he made an issue of it. Or he knew by then that it wasn't such a long shot anymore, that he was going to die, and he didn't want to leave that burden of guilt on his grandson's shoulders. Or make him lose face.

What I told myself, I suppose, was that there'd be other battles, other issues of autonomy and self-expression, other and more serious occasions for these struggles of will and vision. But once you've worked out the calculus of the situation and realized that the sane, humane thing is to give in, the odds have already changed, the tilt of the field has been established, and the occasion never comes up again. Or when something like it does, the terms are even worse, more outrageous and more absurd, so that there seems to be even less point in making an issue.

And was the wedding all that bad? I don't even remember accurately enough to judge. What I seize on is the ridiculous moment just before the ceremony when most of the guests were already seated and the immediate family members were sequestered in the rabbi's study like actors in a green-room waiting to go on. One of Ben's ushers came in to announce that there had been a miscount and that there was still an open seat in the front row on the groom's side. Our side, that is. Irene immediately claimed it, of course, for Albert.

And—yes, I remember now—they were not yet married. I remember how sore I was because Joan, who was my wife, had been excluded, while Albert—Irene's POSSLQ or "significant other" or whatever one calls that relationship these days—was not only there but now was even going to sit with us in the first row.

I could feel the decision forming, not in my head but in the muscles of my thighs, that if he was seated in the front row, I'd walk—out of the room and the door and the city. That recklessness, that determination my father must have had back on that desperate and disagreeable day in the hospital, I now understood. It wasn't anything so planned out and tactical, either, but a compulsion, a need to assert one's dignity and rights or else lose all claim to them.

Albert, though, was tactful and considerate—he and I have always got on quite well, actually—and he declined. "No, I don't think so. It wouldn't be right."

So I could breathe again. And get on with it. Not get through the whole thing, maybe, but see my way to surviving for ten minutes or so.

Which is a lot, sometimes.

The seat stayed empty, Joan's seat, my father's seat.

Which was okay. The vacant chair was not, after all, so pointed a reference to the ugly bickering and ill will on what was supposed to be a happy occasion. In order to read it right, you already had to know all the bad stuff.

I also remember posing for pictures before the ceremony—or I think I do. I've still got some of the pictures, so it's easy to think I'm going all the way back past them to the occasion itself. At any rate, there we all are in standard stilted poses, the family that was coming into being and, in one shot, the family that no longer existed. Nobody looks particularly happy.

I do remember how, after the ceremony, the rabbi whipped off his skullcap, put on his motorcycle helmet, and sped away on a Vespa into the Cambridge traffic. I was surprised and also envious of him, getting away like that, gracefully weaving among the cars and disappearing like a Jewish leprechaun. I still had the reception to get through. All those friends—ex-friends by now, people who had sided with Irene and hadn't spoken to me in years.

I'm being paranoid? Maybe, but it was Irene who had made a point of this business. She was the one who wouldn't talk to people if they talked to me. Or if they had me as a guest in their homes. Or, worst of all, if they talked to Joan. Most of the people we used to know gave in to Irene, perhaps because they thought she was needier than me, or maybe just because they liked her better. That's possible, too, I suppose.

I'm not sniveling. It's not nice, maybe, but it's what people do. But nobody told me this at the time, and I took a lot of it personally. At the wedding reception then, with all of them assembled there in one large room, I felt . . . resentful? suspicious?

No, worse than that. I felt terrible. Whatever my reasons or excuses—my unwillingness to cause pain to my son or my daughter-in-law or to her mother, or to my mother, for that matter—I also was aware that this was not how my father would have behaved. With a noble recklessness, he would have been willing to make a scene, to answer offense with offense, to stalk off if need be, hurting maybe but proud, proud to the death, and unwilling to accept what he considered to be inappropriate behavior. And the costs of this kind of attitude, the terrible costs? He'd have been willing to pay them, as all of us knew who had suffered from our failures to satisfy him. His death a couple of years before Ben's wedding had in no way relaxed his grip on me. If anything, he was more implacable now, a stone figure like the Commendatore in *Don Giovanni* who could never unbend the way a living father sometimes could in a moment of amusement or generosity or grace. The actual man was stern but nowhere near so severe as the idea of him that has remained with me since he died.

Looking at Ben's beard and rubbing my own clean-shaven chin, I thought of him. I wondered whether the fondness that grandparents show their grandchildren would have helped me. If he were gazing down through a painted ceiling of Tintoretto clouds to observe this occasion, would his indulgence to Ben extend to include me? Would he tolerate my toleration for the day's slights and insults? I listened to more or less awkward apologies from some of the wedding guests for the long intervals that had elapsed since their last encounters with me, and I waved an airy hand as if it didn't matter—which was generous and graceful and also the most dismissive thing I could think of to do.

Mostly I managed to keep my feelings concealed so that it looked like a happy enough occasion. There was a band playing, and there were people circulating with drinks and hors d'oeuvres. I danced with the bride and with her mother and with my mother. I allowed myself one drink and then switched to ginger ale.

My foot had gone numb. Some nerve in my left foot

had gone dead on the drive up, as if my body had been voting no, letting me know that this was not a good idea. We shouldn't be doing these things! I should get my foot off the accelerator. My mother's psychosomatic expression had been even more direct: her usual abdominal pains from what she could not stomach. These had kept her from the dinner the night before the wedding. She had gone to bed in her motel room, and I had put in an abbreviated appearance at that prenuptial feast, in no way distressed to have an excuse for an early leave-taking. And again, at the reception, my worry about my mother's health and stamina had allowed us to cut out as soon as the bride and groom had cut the cake.

A day it would be anyway impossible to forget, I have clutched it close, holding onto its images the way some people keep about them a *memento mori*. A steadying counterweight to the extravagances of life's vicissitudes, I can consult it at any time. It is a boulder I have often rolled up the same mountainside. At the thought of it, I can will those tears to flow again that first welled up on the Massachusetts Turnpike from Boston as far as the turnoff for Sturbridge and Connecticut. They are tears not merely of self-pity but of helplessness, of a victim who cannot control the terrifying struggles raging about him—for I am not only the father of the groom but also a young child, perhaps five or six years old, whose parents are shouting at each other and who is helpless, afraid for each of them, afraid for himself, unable to choose between them, and also unable to nudge them toward any reconciliation. Caught between my son and my mother and my own inclinations, or between their promptings and those of my father, I am powerless, terrified, and feel altogether worthless in a way that would have delighted Irene, if only she had known about it.

Easy to say this, of course, but it was not easy to understand it and puzzle it out. It took years, long nights of bad dreams and fitful daytime forays into that bewitched territory. My mother is dead too now, but the fight goes on, the rages and the yelling, and the little boy inside me who peers out from his hiding place is still likely to be spooked by loud noises or threatening displays of emotion.

How little I have accomplished in six years! I am somewhat more aware of some of these foibles of mine, but I still worry that the baby will be a boy, in which case there will be a *bris* I shall have to attend. The cast and crew of the old melodrama will be reassembled for an additional scene or two.

New thrills and chills! New humiliations and tortures!

Of course, it is a boy.

I have been doing what sometimes works, mentally rehearsing for encounters I'll have to face so I'll be prepared for all eventualities. No one on the plane could guess the reason for my trip. An observer would suppose that I am either a professor or an executive in one of those professorial industries—computer programming, perhaps. I don't look like a grandfather.

But I don't feel like one, either. Grandfathers should be wise or at least mature enough not to have to play such childish games with themselves, trying to whistle up their courage to face specters and phantoms that are mostly of their own invention. When he is old enough to talk, what will I be able to tell my grandson, what assurance will I have for him? It is not enough to nod one's head and say, "You know, those awful fears you have, uh, are absolutely justified. If anything, you underestimate the menace. If you want to know, I'm more frightened than you are."

Some grandpa I'm going to be. Am!

The plane lands. For once in my life, I don't grip the arms of the seat in an attempt to control my terror. I have the feeling that my life is running smoothly but almost entirely out of my control. I am a passive creature on a conveyor belt where imps and demons operate grotesque machinery. It is the feeling I have in a hospital when I am wheeled along on a gurney, watching ceiling tiles and overhead lights flash past me. But what could happen that would be worse than what I have already imagined?

Never ask such a question! There's always an answer. In this case, I am to be the *sandek,* which is a great honor. I'd forgotten that part. Or I had assumed that Irene's father would be the *sandek,* being the child's great-grandfather, his only living great-grandparent and, at eighty, the patriarch. But he's in the Caribbean on a cruise Irene didn't want to interrupt. So I am the *sandek,* which means that I hold the baby while the *moyel* does his job.

It is a greater honor even than being a godparent. And impossible to refuse. But my God! I am terrified at the idea of it. What if I faint at the sight of blood? I don't know whether this is likely or not. I have never had such an experience and have no way of guessing. I am relieved to hear that I don't have to do what Irene's grandfather did at Ben's *bris,* which was actually hold the baby in his lap. This *moyel* works at a bridge table at which I will be seated with my feet on a phone book so my knees touch the bottom of the table. The baby is therefore still in my lap, at least in a sacramental way, but I'm less likely to drop him.

I am not altogether reassured. The precaution is not one that would have been introduced without any demonstrable need, so I cannot help imagining hundreds of *sandeks* passing out and letting all those eight-day-old babies slip to the floor. I am tempted to try to get out of it, but what would my father say? Or my mother, for that matter? I have been thinking how pleased she'd have been, had it been given her to survive to this day. She'd have come back from a cruise—or would never have been on one at a time when a birth was impending.

Joan is here. Irene is here. Claire, Ruth's mother, is here. They are all talking together amicably. I am able to greet the young people, Ruth and Ben's friends, to whom I am introduced. And I am able to shake hands or kiss some of the older ones, those who used to be my friends and were such torments at the wedding. I don't care so much anymore. Our lives have gone on.

The beginnings of grandfatherly wisdom? Perhaps so, but that's nothing to be proud of. At most, it is a sense of proportion, an awareness of larger griefs. On top of the bookcase, along with the wedding pictures, there are Ben's photographs of my mother and father. And there's a picture of me, clowning a little in a straw hat. I'm smiling in the photograph and maybe ten pounds lighter than I am now, so my connection with that image is indirect and somewhat wistful.

The *moyel* is ready. I sit where I'm told to sit. He explains how the baby will be passed from the mother to the various people who are to be honored and then will be placed for a moment on the empty chair, Elijah's chair, and then at last will be handed to me. He asks before us all for Ben's authorization to perform the circumcision. Ben says yes. There are prayers in Hebrew. The baby is handed about like a package and arrives all too quickly to me. I am required to hold his thighs apart, pressing them down—quite hard, actually, because his thigh muscles are strong—onto the tabletop. More Hebrew. The *moyel* asks Ben to repeat some blessing, and Ben does so but with difficulty. He can hardly get the words out. Irene is at the table beside me, with a rubber nipple that has been dipped in a little Concord grape sacramental wine, the sweet stuff I used to like when I was a child.

The *moyel* pulls back the foreskin with a forceps, and I close my eyes tightly. I am pressing hard on the baby's thighs. I can't wipe away any of the sweat that has erupted on my face. It's hot in here—Ben has turned up the thermostat for the baby's sake—but it isn't the heat that's making me sweat. It's this barbarous business! I can't believe I'm doing this to another human being, let alone to my own grandson. Grandfathers are supposed to be softies; they're supposed to enjoy some special bond with their grandchildren. Presents and fun, adoration and kisses are supposed to issue from grandparents, not pain. Relent, relent, I iterate in silence in an unbeliever's desperate prayer. We could perhaps all change our minds and become Lutherans or Methodists or bland Congregationalists, for Christ's sake. How much longer can this awfulness continue? I peep, see the bloodied glans, and close my eyes again, tighter than ever. The baby is crying, and from behind me I can hear that Ruth is crying, too.

And then I hear in my left ear Irene's crooning: "It's all right, baby. It's okay. It's okay, baby." Over and over, as a desperate prayer. "It'll be okay. It's all right, baby."

I breathe in time to her short, slow sentences. I know she's talking to the baby, but I am soothed as if it were me she were addressing, as if it were all okay, as if nothing terrible had happened or was happening, as if everything had always been all right and she could still address me lovingly that way, as if those were my own mother's sobs I was hearing, as if it would all be, as she promised, okay.

And then the *moyel* says, "Mazel tov," and it's all over. I can let go. I open my eyes.

They wrap the baby in his blanket. Miraculously, he stops crying.

There are more prayers. They name the boy Isaac, for Ruth's father. It means "laughter," God's laughter at Abraham and Sarah's despair.

A good name. There are toasts now. To life, and to Isaac. People congratulate me.

"I didn't do anything," I say, lying.

Hurricane Charlie

It had rained most of the way up, sometimes hard enough to slow the traffic to a crawl, occasionally with a crazy force that reduced visibility to just a few feet and resounded on the roof of the car like small-arms fire. But Bernie had pushed on, eager to get to the next punctuation mark in the long trip: the Rhode Island line, the turnoff at Providence for 195, the Sagamore Bridge, and then the exit he used to take from Route 6.

A tough trip—and not just physically. It wasn't easy driving by what had once been his house and now was Dorothy's and seeing that it was in need of painting and that the juniper needed to be clipped back. None of his business now. He wasn't allowed inside, as a matter of fact. That was Dorothy's rule. Okay, it was her house, but the kids would all be there together, and that didn't happen very often.

But Maggie's place was just down the street, and Bernie would still have a chance to see them. It wasn't ideal, but it was better than nothing. To see the kids, he had decided it would be worth putting up with a few minor and predictable assaults.

The storm was just one more nuisance, an inconvenience he hadn't been able to foresee, but now that he'd arrived safely, he welcomed it as an accurate expression of his mood. Tourists hated rain, having come up for their expensive two weeks and wanting every moment of their time to be perfect. This kind of weather drove them into the used-book barns and antique stores and the cute shoppes that sold baskets to people who didn't need them but couldn't think of what else to do with themselves in bad weather on Cape Cod. Baskets they bought, and bayberry candles.

Bernie wasn't a tourist. He had lived here, year-round, for years and had spilled serious tears when he'd left. For the end of the marriage and the death of the family, but for the place, too, for the land itself and its weather, sometimes soft, often somber, and on occasion distraught, as it was now.

He was sitting in Maggie's living room, dealing a game of patience on the top of what he recognized as a table that used to be his. Dorothy had given it to Maggie. There were other items in Maggie's house that he recognized. In the guest bedroom where he'd put his suitcase, the dresser was part of a set that had been his and Dorothy's. In the dining room, there was an oak server he'd picked up at a Saturday night auction and had always liked a lot. Dorothy had given it away.

Well, okay. She could do what she wanted with all that stuff. She'd turned Bernie's old study into a billiard room, just to defile it, just to obliterate whatever of his spirit might have lingered there.

A gust of wind and intensified rain sounded outside and fluttered the leaves of a stand of birch trees, showing their light undersides. A strong wind. Not so bad—so far—as the wind of '54 that took down a lot of old trees and blew off a fair number of roofs. But who could say what was going to happen this time? Right now, there was a hurricane watch. The storm was somewhere off the Jersey shore, and there were a lot of things it could do—peter out, get stronger, head out to sea, or keep on course up the shore toward the Cape. It was hard not to want that to happen, to welcome it. Bernie remembered how in '66 he'd done all the right things, putting tape up on the windowpanes and swamping the boat in Round Cove. Then the storm had turned tail and scampered away, leaving him unharmed but also feeling dumb. All that work for nothing! Bernie had felt stupid, the way the righteous men and women of Sodom would have felt if there had been eleven or twelve of them.

In a theoretical way, Bernie approved of these big storms, the huge brooms God sent to sweep away the work of impudent builders of summer homes and resorts on land that stuck out vulnerably into the ocean and got hit every so often by rough weather. The Cape and the Keys—they were both cleaned off every now and then, only to have the people come sneaking back, fishermen and campers first with their modest shacks, and then venturesome proprietors of bait shops that grew into general stores, and sooner or later a few simple motel operators. After a while, all memory of the disaster faded, and the developers of the luxury condos and swank resorts descended to defy the elements once again.

A dark day and a dark mood. Bernie played with the limp Cape Cod cards. It was the dampness. Cape Cod salt cellars always had rice in them for this dampness. Bernie was waiting for his daughter to drop by. To grace him with the favor of her presence. He'd arrived at Maggie's Sunday afternoon, having left almost at dawn to get here before Esther and Daniel and Aaron left. His daughter-in-law and his son and grandson had to get back to Boston, but they had delayed their departure and braved the bad weather and Sunday evening traffic up Route 3 to come down to Maggie's so that Bernie could at least see the six-month-old infant and watch him get fed his strained peaches or sweet potatoes, or whatever that yellow-orange goo had been. It seemed to be nourishing, anyway. The kid had great Sidney Greenstreet jowls. And rolls of fat from his wrists up his arms, like the Michelin man who is made out of tires.

It had been wonderful seeing them, but the contrast

was burdensome. Where had Emily been? Why hadn't she come by, too?

It was no good keeping score. That only enraged him, and he knew it. Still, if he were to work it out, the time Emily spent with him would come to maybe a tenth of the time she spent with Dorothy. He resisted that kind of arithmetic because it would only make him feel terrible. He'd gone through the rationalizations often enough—about how Dorothy lived in attractive places, down in the Florida Keys and up here in what had once been their house on Cape Cod. (True, granted, and yet irrelevant! These kids were grown up now. They should understand that it wasn't a contest between their mother and father as to which could contrive the more attractive trap, set up the more appealing vacation spot, or offer gaudier toys in a battle for their attention and loyalty and love. To hell with that!)

He heard the door opening, the one in the kitchen that stuck a little from the dampness, and he called out, "Emily?"

"She hasn't come by?"

It was Maggie. She had gone to fetch dinner. And also to leave Bernie alone to have time with his daughter.

"No," Bernie said.

She shrugged. "We should eat. I got some fried clams and onion rings. There's no white wine, but we've got red. Or vodka."

"Either one."

They ate. Maggie was one of the very few people who had been able to remain friends with both Bernie and Dorothy. Dorothy had generally insisted that people choose between them, but Maggie had refused to do that. And she had managed to get away with it, too—at first because Bernie was Rob's godfather. And then, after Rob's accident, because grief of that magnitude was intimidating. Even to Dorothy.

Maggie had had Rob brought up the week before by

ambulance, with his nurse and her daughter. He'd been shipped back to the hospital on Friday. When Bernie arrived a couple of days later, he had, of course, asked what Rob's visit had been like. Maggie said it went fine. But she also admitted she hadn't been able to tell for sure if Rob knew where he was. He recognized her, she thought. She was a familiar face and voice. But whether he knew that she was his mother was another question.

Still another question, and probably the toughest of all, was what to hope for. If Rob was out of it so that he knew only what a dog or a cat knows, familiar faces and being warm and dry and comfortable, that was tough to bear but tolerable. But what if there was more? What if he knew who he was and who Maggie was? What if there was an intelligence trapped in that uncontrollable and inexpressive body? What then? Bernie decided he'd rather be dead than in that pitiable condition. And Maggie's plight was surely almost that bad.

The accident had happened almost three years ago. The first month or two, the question had seemed simpler, whether Rob would live or die, whether the swelling of the brain could be controlled or not. If the traumatized tissue continued to swell, the neurosurgeons explained, there was the danger that it would press down through the opening in the base of the skull and destroy itself.

It hadn't done that, though. A triumph of medical science. Or a disaster.

From Maggie's responses, Bernie gathered that she agreed with him—in part. Or that a part of her agreed with him. Another part of her kept hoping that somehow or other, even after the passage of all this time, there would be some connection Rob might still learn to make with his old life.

Yes and *no* would be good for a start.

Twenty-two years old, and he was eating baby food and

wearing diapers. Or, on good days, he could eat baby food—until the effort of swallowing exhausted him and he fell asleep. They pumped hyperalimentation into his stomach at night to keep him alive. They had been doing so well with it that Maggie worried about Rob's being overweight. She was convinced that he recognized people. She thought his sign for that was to raise his eyebrows. But it wasn't reliable. It could also signal the start of a yawn.

Bernie had worked it out so that he would arrive after Rob was taken away. It was too depressing. He'd seen Rob in various hospitals and at various stages of his stabilization (one could hardly call it a recovery). The doctors said that even if he were somehow to put together some new connections in his head, he would still be unable to recall certain details—the last year of his life, for instance. Olivia, his girlfriend, had been with him in the car. She'd been luckier. She'd been killed instantly.

They had both been drinking, and according to the state police report, the car had been going at least seventy miles an hour on a foggy night on a winding country road.

Dumb, but that's what kids do, Bernie thought. They think they are immortal.

Or, no. Not dumb, he corrected himself. Stupid. Now Rob was dumb. The last thing Bernie wanted to do was to hurt Maggie by thoughtlessly using the wrong word.

They finished the fried clams and onion rings. They had drunk vodka syrupy from the freezer as their table wine. The dishes were not much of a chore: paper plates into the garbage and the two tumblers into the dishwasher. Or, on second thought, they decided to hold onto the tumblers. The vodka could also substitute for brandy and cordials.

Bernie meanwhile invented more excuses for Emily. He persuaded himself that Dorothy must have planned a big dinner, something special that Emily hadn't wanted to miss.

Or something she couldn't miss without giving offense. But as soon as dinner was over, she'd come on down. That was it, of course. And it stood to reason that if she was coming down for a nice long chat after dinner, it wouldn't have made much sense for her to come before.

Yes, of course. He'd been a fool to worry about why she hadn't shown up right away. There was enough suffering in the world without inventing more.

"Coffee?" Maggie asked.

"No, not unless you're having some. This is just fine," Bernie said, raising his glass and smiling cheerfully.

They went into the living room and sat down on the porch furniture with which Maggie had improvised. On a gorgeous day when sunshine streamed in through the windows, it more or less worked. On a gray day or a dank evening like this one, it was just porch furniture in a living room—sad and out of place. There was a maple couch on which Bernie sprawled, still tired from the drive up. Maggie sat in one of her Adirondack chairs and hit him with her idea, which, she admitted, might sound a little bit crazy.

"Who's more entitled to craziness?" he asked, as a way of encouraging her.

"I was talking with Carole last week," she said. Carole was a young woman who had once been in one of Dorothy's English classes. Dorothy had spotted her as a bright youngster and picked her out to do something with, inviting her to baby-sit for Daniel and Emily and in a more general way befriending her. Carole had wanted to study home economics at one of the Massachusetts state teachers' colleges, but Dorothy had raised her sights and widened her horizons so that she went to New York and studied economics at Hunter, living with Maggie in the spare room of her apartment in exchange for baby-sitting Rob and being a mother's helper.

"She's thirty-seven now, you know," Maggie said.

"Oh?"

"And she's thinking about having a child. Not getting

married, but just having a child. All her beaux seem to be married men."

"Well, women are doing that," Bernie said, thinking about how words like *beaux* were relics of Maggie's childhood in the South.

"I asked her whether she might not want to have a child by Rob," Maggie said. "Assuming that they can get sperm from him. I could still be a grandmother that way. And she'd know who the father was, although he wouldn't know . . ."

Bernie didn't know what to say. He took a sip of vodka, but that only bought him a few seconds.

"You think it's crazy?" Maggie asked.

"What did Carole think?"

"Her first reaction was that it would be too much like incest. But she's considering it. She's given herself this year, which is reasonable, I guess."

"So you could be a grandmother?"

"Exactly," Maggie said, nodding seriously.

"Well, it's no crazier than anything else," Bernie said. "If Carole wants to have a child anyway, I don't see what's wrong with it. I wouldn't push it, though."

"Oh, no. Of course not."

They were quiet for a while. Then Bernie asked a question almost as delicate. "You think Carole's happier this way than she would have been if we'd all just left her alone?"

"I don't know," Maggie said. "I asked her that myself once. She didn't know. She didn't think she'd want to give up all the intellectual advantages, the cultural pleasures she's learned to take for granted. Or be willing to trade them. But happier? What is happiness? Who knows?"

Then, after a moment's thought, she said, "She doesn't blame Dorothy, though. Or any of us. It wasn't all that one-sided. She collaborated. She agreed. She was flattered by Dorothy's attention. And yours and mine."

"I guess so." Bernie looked at his watch. It was after

83

nine. Emily wasn't coming. "I'm exhausted from the long drive," he said, to apologize to Maggie for looking at the time. And to suggest—to her? to himself?—that maybe it was a good thing Emily hadn't come over. He'd see her tomorrow. They'd have plenty of time together.

And there would be time also to talk with Maggie about this crazy plan of hers to become a grandmother. Science fiction, it sounded like. But they do weird things, those doctors. Keeping Rob alive, for instance.

Up in the guest bedroom, Bernie lay down in the darkness and tried to sleep, but the room was warm and close. He got up and opened the window a little so he could feel the bite of the storm outside. It might rain in a little, but there was nothing of value to be damaged. He lay down again and listened to the intermittent tirades and lulls of the wind in the leaves of the tall trees. Like people screaming at each other. Or ghosts of old arguments, the words and sense of which were long gone but the passions of which still raged, as in one of the circles of Dante's hell.

In the morning he expected she'd call. Of course she'd call. Maggie invited Bernie to go out and look at bathroom fixtures with her. She was going to redo the bathroom at long last, and she didn't know anything about tubs and sinks and commodes.

What was there to know? She was playing the southern belle, the dependent female who needs the advice of a strong and knowing male. She was also offering him an alternative to hanging in limbo and waiting for the phone to ring. A way to defer for the morning the unpleasant truth that was already obvious to her . . .

Or was he being paranoid? It was tough to decide about his own sanity.

He declined her invitation with thanks. He'd just hang around and read a little. There wasn't anything he could tell her about fixtures. And, no, there wasn't anything he needed.

He heard the door close behind her, the sound of the car's engine, and then nothing but the sluice of water from one of the downspouts onto a piece of slate. He sprawled on the sofa and tried to marshal his spirits, aware that he needed to be on the alert, realizing that he was likely to collapse. He'd been here nearly eighteen hours now, and she had not come by. Hadn't even called.

Passive-aggressive behavior? Punishment still for his having left her mother, for his having gone out for that year to California?

Worse than that, it was probably just thoughtlessness. Inattention. Indifference. The word was part of a Mauriac title, or was it one by Moravia? It was the *M*'s that made it confusing. Bernie had been at a dinner party a few months before when the woman to his left had mentioned Lake Perry. In northern Italy. He'd thought for a moment, managed not to laugh, and asked her if she didn't mean Lake Como.

Without getting too psychiatric, he supposed that the worst part of this was being left alone and having no control over his situation. It was like being an infant who has no sure sense when his mother leaves that she will ever come back and who is bereaved each time as if she had died. He was being made to relive that inconsolable grief of being abandoned.

Good! To get it all out that way in the light of day was healthy and good. The catch was that this only made it harder to forgive Emily. If he could see this, why couldn't she? It wasn't through any deficiency of intellect. It went back to the original difficulty—a failure of attention. A lack of concern that a stranger would have the right to resent and that a father should never have to experience.

He thought about Goriot. And Lear. Bernie didn't suppose he was in any way immune to their domestic difficulties, but he felt himself to be protected simply because he didn't have their scope and scale. He was a mere dabbler in distress. All he had to do was look around, look at Maggie, for instance, and see what she had to bear.

She'd had a ramp built to get Rob's wheelchair up from ground level and in through the front door. And there were angled pieces of wood on some of the thresholds so the wheels could roll over them more easily. Now that Rob had been shipped back to the hospital, she'd had the ramp taken down and stored in the garage, but the grass that had been underneath it was yellowed. This rain might green it up some, Bernie supposed.

He turned on the radio and hunted for a weather report. The storm had turned east somewhere off south Jersey and was going away from land. The rain would continue for a while, but there would be clearing in the afternoon. That was comforting. He was not Lear, not worth blowing winds and spouting cataracts and hurricanoes.

To hell with pride. He had told himself he wouldn't call and that it was her place to call him. But he hadn't told her that. Maybe she was sitting by the phone up there waiting for him to call her, not sure whether he was awake yet. That was plausible, although just barely. He picked up the phone and called what had once been his own number. At the worst, Dorothy would answer, and he'd ask for Emily, calmly and matter-of-factly. But he didn't even have to do that. Emily herself answered.

"You're up?" he asked.

"Oh, yeah."

"Well, what's the plan?"

"I'm going off this morning with Mom to buy sneakers."

He was silent for a moment. "I've been here, waiting for you," he said. Calm, calm, he told himself.

86

"We'll see each other. This afternoon. As soon as I get back. I'll call you."

"For lunch?"

"Say, right after."

"Say, between twelve and two?"

"Okay."

"I'll be waiting."

"Lighten up, Dad, will you? I'll call."

"By two!"

"Okay."

He hung up. Better that than a tirade.

Maggie came back, annoyed at the estimate she'd been given—eight thousand dollars! On the other hand, their idea for what to do with the bathroom was sensible. Put the tub on the wall where the sink was and build an enclosing wall. And put the vanity where the tub was. That would be a way around the problem of that slanting ceiling from the gable that overhung the bathtub. Bernie told her he thought it sounded sensible. Why not take that idea to another plumber and see if she could get better numbers? Or a plumber and a carpenter? That way, she would be the contractor herself and would be hiring subcontractors. It was more nuisance that way, but she'd save money.

She said she'd try that and asked if he'd had lunch.

He shook his head.

"Emily coming down?"

"She's got some errands to run. She'll call me when she gets back," Bernie said. He realized that he was covering up, but was it for his daughter or himself? Or was it for Maggie's sake, not wanting to burden her further with his trivial annoyances?

"We could go out, but the traffic's awful. Everybody's just driving up and down Route 28. Or we've got tuna fish. And bread."

87

"Tuna fish is fine," he said.

They made tuna fish sandwiches. She put lemon juice in the tuna fish salad, and onion and green pepper along with the celery. She said the lemon juice was to kill the fishy taste. Bernie didn't allow himself to ask her why, if she didn't want a fishy taste, she was using tuna fish. That was why someone thought up chicken salad.

They sat down at the counter together to eat their sandwiches. "Well," she asked, "What do you think? About my crazy idea?"

"The bathroom idea or the grandmother idea?"

She smiled, acknowledging the joke.

He shook his head. "I think it's up to Carole, really. But that's beside the point. You mean what do I think myself."

She nodded again.

"I don't know. I thought about it. I thought about Aaron. And Daniel and Emily. And what I think about the world. It's getting to be close to a quarter of a million dollars to get a kid through good schools. Which is crazy. Maybe people will figure out how crazy it is. There's a point beyond which it isn't even economical. You take what it costs to send a kid to prep school and college and graduate or professional school and give it to him when he's in the eighth grade—and he can retire. Never even touch capital. Just live on the income in Guadalajara or on some Greek island and be the richest guy in the village. What sense does that make?"

"Easy for you to say, now that you're through it."

"You're never through it."

"I am," she said instantly.

There was no answer to that.

After lunch, Maggie said she was going to put on her slicker and walk on the beach, which looked wonderful when there was a storm. Especially now, when the storm wasn't dangerous anymore. Did he want to come?

He said he'd wait for Emily's call.

That was when he got out the cards and started to play solitaire. Patience, it was called. He didn't cheat, but he allowed himself to go back through the deck by threes as often as he could, which was as liberal an interpretation of the rules as there was.

At one-thirty, he realized there was a possibility that she might not call. And that he'd then have to choose between humiliation (which there would be either way) and fury. Which emotion was worse in the long run? Maybe the humiliation would be better, more dramatic and instructive. She'd feel bad, wouldn't she, if he just got in the car and drove home?

But after a while it wasn't what she'd feel but what he'd feel. At least he wouldn't be sitting here, waiting like a dope. He'd be putting miles between himself and this pain, this disaster area.

At two o'clock, he put the cards away and went up to pack. He could give her the time it would take to get his things together and into the trunk. Another ten minutes or so. She had promised to call by two.

He could imagine waiting, swallowing his pride, as bitter as bile. She'd come by—at three, maybe, or three-thirty. But she'd come eventually. And they could pretend it hadn't happened, that he hadn't sat around for twenty-four hours like a minor courtier at Versailles . . .

He could imagine someone doing that. But not him. Someone else.

Like a zombie, with that stiffness and clumsiness, he put clothes into his suitcase. He got his Dopp kit from the bathroom. He grabbed the little attaché case that held the tapes for the cassette player he kept on the front seat when he drove. He wrote out a note for Maggie: "Can't stand it anymore. Sorry I can't be more help to you. I can't even help myself!"

Then he got into the car and drove up Bank Street and

back to the Mid-Cape Highway, afraid now that he might see Dorothy and Emily coming back from their important appointment to buy sneakers together. It would ruin the drama of it to be seen and intercepted and perhaps prevented.

He put a Mozart piano concerto into the tape player and let it wash over him, a soothing liquid, an elixir of sanity and decency and order.

In Buzzard's Bay he stopped to fill the tank and looked up to see that the sky was clearing. As they'd said it would. The sun was coming out. A lot nature knows, he decided, squinting up.

He'd call Maggie in a day or two, he decided. And then, thinking about her, he realized that he couldn't advise her about her crazy idea. He couldn't tell her what he really thought—which was unspeakable and terrible but true. In a way, she was lucky. Luckier than he. Rob was a wreck, a ruin, but he had been restored to her, diapers and baby food and all, as the loyal and dependent creature who never talks back and causes no pain.

After that, it's all downhill.

Simple Justice

Our first dog was an Airedale named Sparky. Or Flashy. One of those.

I don't remember the dog. I was an infant. What I do remember is my mother's stories of her surprise at how the dog kept on growing bigger and bigger until he could grab food from the kitchen table. Until he was strong enough to drag her helplessly along after him whenever she took him out.

It was crazy for my parents to have picked an Airedale, but what did either of them know about dogs? Neither one ever had a childhood pet. But now they had a baby—me—and their idea must have been that the pattern would be complete if they got a dog, too.

Husband, wife, baby, and dog.

They would have discussed it together, adding other reasons, sensible reasons, such as the added safety there would be for my mother and me if there was a watchdog in the house. But they would have done it for the unreasonable reason, the picture they had in their heads of what their life was supposed to look like.

They couldn't stand the dog, though. Airedales are lively and active and noisy and huge. They gave the dog away to Manny Endlich, who had a place out in the country somewhere near Peekskill. He kept goats. He had a pretty wife and no children.

I remember visiting the Endlichs. It was the first time I ever saw goats. And it was also the first time I ever saw ripe olives—which look like goat shit.

And I remember our 1938 or 1939 black Plymouth with a kind of leatherette roof and running boards. I remember how the Plymouth bounced on the dirt road to the Endlichs.

But I don't remember the Airedale. By the time I was old enough to have anything like a coherent recollection of these visits, the Airedale was dead. And the Endlichs had a wire-haired fox terrier named Flashy. Or Sparky. Whichever the Airedale wasn't.

The trick, though, may be not to pay too close attention, to see things without looking too hard. What difference does it make if you get the details wrong, red or green, May or November?

Probably my first clear and indubitable memory is of pain. My left ear aches. I am on a bus. A red bus. My mother and I are on our way back from Los Angeles. I am crying. My crying is so unrelenting and loud that the bus stops and we get out. We return to Los Angeles. My hearing is still deficient in that ear, the left ear. There was an infection, and the eardrum was perforated. It is remarkable to think that they didn't have antibiotics then. I'm not even sure that there were sulfa drugs.

What did not strike me as remarkable—or not at the time, anyway—was that my mother and I should cross the country to visit my aunt and uncle. Why not? Adults do huge and epic things quite normally. If you are allowed to cross the street, why not cross the continent?

On the other hand, in that memory we are on a bus. I remember we were on a train on the way out. But we were taking a bus back.

Only much later did it dawn on me that that trip, the visit to my aunt and uncle, was a deliberate separation. My mother had left my father. And the return was a trial reconciliation. Which explains, in those depression days, the trip west in the relative luxury of high dudgeon—on the train— while the trip back would have been more deliberate and restrained, both in spirit and expense.

I remember seeing a photograph of the little park in Los Angeles where my cousin and I posed in front of the miniature houses that had been set up for the Seven Dwarfs from Walt Disney's film, which was just opening. It is playing again now in its fiftieth anniversary run.

I may have the photograph somewhere, but I don't need it. I remember how I look, in that determined, commercial cheeriness. I have big ears and look very serious. Sad, really.

My mother is not in the photograph. She may have been holding the camera, an old Kodak box camera of the kind you still sometimes see in junk shops.

The reconciliation worked out. They stayed together, at any rate. And to celebrate or seal that, or maybe just to fulfill that pattern of perfection they still were trying to achieve but that hadn't worked out with the dog, they had another child. My sister.

Mom, Dad, brother, and sister.

This is like archaeology. The shards that remain are pathetically small and almost grudging; the leaps one must make are dizzying; the surmises are precarious. But the enterprise is thrilling because of those great distances. Childhood is an age when giants tread the earth. Look at a child crossing the street, flanked by creatures three times his size. These huge beings are benevolent, mostly.

But not always.

I remember my children holding my hand and their mother's, walking between us, holding on tight and swinging for the fun of it and also to determine, once again, that we could be trusted. That we wouldn't drop them.

I think I remember having done that myself.

Holding my parents together. That too.

The arrival of a sister would have been welcome, then. More glue. More cement.

There must have been rivalry, too, I suppose, but I don't remember that. I don't recall any resentment or fear about being supplanted as the adored creature in the heart of that household. I'm afraid the reason I didn't feel much of a threat was that I didn't take my sister seriously. I was never quite convinced that she was real, a person, an independent center of consciousness.

I would have been hard put, at four, to formulate such an idea. But it seems to me now that the besetting difficulty we always had—Mom, Dad, Sis, and I—was acknowledging one another as centers of consciousness. Each of us treated the others as projections or implements.

One of Kant's categorical imperatives is that each person must be viewed as an end in himself and not as a means to the ends of others.

This is a lot tougher and more demanding than the Golden Rule.

But my parents were using her, had created her as a bond between them, a trophy of their reunion.

She was a substitute for Sparky or Flashy.

They were using me, too, although it took me a while to find that out.

I was a little kid and didn't know anything. Little kids don't know much. They look around and put together bits of information, drawing conclusions that seem reasonable to them, but they make mistakes. They have to keep reinventing the wheel, which is not so easy. The Aztecs invented the wheel but somehow never realized that they could make big wheels move large loads. They put little wheels on toys, and that's all.

They thought wheels were funny.

I thought laughter was the opposite of yelling.

There was a lot of yelling. I don't remember about what, but they yelled—at each other, at Sis, at me. Whatever problems they'd had before the separation must have still been there. They yelled, which used to scare me. And they laughed. Dad had a sense of humor. He told jokes, but more than that, he found things to laugh at. Sometimes he roared with laughter. And Mom laughed with him.

That wasn't scary. That was like having them hold on while I lifted my feet off the pavement and swung like a little ape with its mama and papa apes in the jungle.

I guess a lot of children must think that. They're the ones who grow up to be comedians, the ones who deal with terror by making jokes. On the gurney on the way into an operating room, they're cracking wise and making the nurses laugh. As if that would ensure a decent outcome in there.

I learned to make my parents laugh. I learned to make Sis laugh, too. That was easier. I could tickle her and she'd laugh. Just like that. Like a little toy. Which is what I thought she was.

Her earliest memory is of our playing, horsing around one way or another, and my doing something to make her cry. And then I'd tickle her to get her to laugh.

Sometimes I'd tickle her so much, she'd pee in her pants. And she'd still be laughing.

That was funny, too, I thought.

She'd try to call Mom and Dad at the office, and I'd let her dial all the digits but one. Then I'd put my thumb on the dingus on the cradle that cuts the connection. And she'd bawl.

And I'd tickle her and she'd laugh again.

She hated that. She still hates the memory of it, which is as vivid for her as my memory of that earache.

95

Yes, I'm sorry about it. I can see how it was wrong. But I was seven, maybe eight years old. What did I know?

I knew what I'd picked up, what I'd pieced together. Yelling and crying were bad. Laughter was good.

Both of those propositions are still true. What's false is the idea that laughter is the opposite of yelling and crying, that it can cancel them out.

It wasn't that I was such a dopey kid. I was smart, I guess. Smart enough anyway to be bored in school, which was why I got disappointing report cards. Not all As. A fair number of Bs and even, in Citizenship or Deportment or whatever they called it, Cs. I remember one of my teachers in the fourth or fifth grade asking what was mined in the tin mines of Bolivia, and my disbelief that it could be a serious question.

"Oranges," I answered.

The class laughed a lot. The teacher didn't. I got another C in Citizenship.

My father told me that unless I tried harder, I'd never get into Old Siwash.

It never even occurred to me that I might not want to go to Old Siwash.

My father had gone there. More to the point, my father had started there. And then, when his father had died, he had had to drop out and finish at night at State, at the city campus. Instead of the Gothic towers and the ivy and the drinking songs, there were subways and trolleys and a daytime job in the title company.

It was the great disappointment of his life. And instead of hating Siwash for having done this to him, he decided he'd get married and have a son, and the son could go there and get the degree he'd been cheated out of. He'd beat them at their own game.

Only they weren't playing any games. There wasn't even anybody around who remembered him.

96

But he gave money to the alumni fund every year. He was sure they kept track of these things. And he got married and had a son. And he taught me to sing all the Old Siwash songs.

> Oogle boogle, oogle boogle,
> Oogle boogle, oogle boogle,
> Oogle boogle, oogle boogle,
> Old Siwash . . . we love you.

This is, admittedly, a stupid song. Aggressively so. Like "Boola boola" that the Yalies sing. But it has a tradition, and they're proud of it.

My father used to sing this with me on his knee. We used to sing it together.

My sister was jealous as hell because he never sang it with her.

Siwash didn't take girls then, so it never occurred to him to get her fired up about going there. She wasn't part of his scheme.

She hated to be excluded.

Eventually I hated to be included. I hated being a toy.

Like Sparky. Like Sis.

The thing about Siwash is that my father hated it when he was there. It was a terribly snotty place—it still is, in some respects—and not at all comfortable for a Jewish kid from the city, which is what he was. It was a part of his revenge fantasy that his son would be one of those suave preppies who, from the very first day, walked around as if they owned the place. Which meant that I had to go to prep school.

Given the fact that I was bored in public school and didn't have many friends there, I was pleased with the idea of going away to school. I could start fresh, turn over a new leaf, have lots of friends, and enjoy interesting teachers.

We went around and looked at a number of schools.

But St. Pederast had the classiest reputation. Two vice-presidents went there, and three members of the Supreme Court. A long time ago, but that was just what my father liked. Ivy, Georgian buildings, and traditions.

It wasn't fun. Even a new leaf has some connection to the book in which it appears.

This isn't a prep school story. I have it in mind to write one someday. It will tell quite simply and directly what kinds of things they used to do at St. Pederast. How the masters used to carry side arms, and if they could catch you violating the rules—drinking or driving a car or smoking or not making your bed—they'd shoot you. Shoot to wound, the first time. And then, on the second offense, shoot to kill.

It was tough, but it was fair. And if it didn't cripple you or kill you, it made a man of you.

Look at Vice-President Fairbanks. At Vice-President Wheeler. At Mr. Justice Blatchford. At John W. Weeks, secretary of war under President Harding. And their portraits, all of them with a great deal of varnish, are hanging on the wall in Weir Hall—which we used to call Weird Hall, naturally—so you can do just that.

The portraits could as easily be those of robber barons or undertakers for all most of the parents know or care. What parents like about the school is that it has a reputation for getting kids into Yale and Harvard.

And Princeton and Dartmouth and Amherst and Old Siwash.

Oogle boogle!

Not that Sis did so badly on the deal. Dad may not have had any fantasies about her academic career, but what he arranged for her was the best there was. If only out of fairness. She went off to Upscale Country Day School and then to Toplofty. Nothing slouch about either of those. But what she remembers is all those dinner table conversations at home in which Dad would ask me—would grill me, actually—about my day in school. And she'd try to come in for her share of attention with her little triumphs, but he'd never respond in the same way. Her grades were better than mine, but that didn't count.

He listened. He wasn't altogether crazy. But it wasn't part of his plan.

She had no idea how lucky she was.

Which of us ever does?

We grew up. Kids grow up and move out. Some of the inevitable quarrels of adolescence may have been avoided because we were away at boarding schools. Or they may have been saved up for summer vacations. I remember I ran away from home one summer and got as far as Washington, D.C., but I couldn't find work washing dishes or busing tables, which is how I'd planned to get around the country. I called up, had them wire money, and came home.

Sis had her own way of rebelling, which was to wait a while and only make her bet when she was holding the right cards.

Getting married was one such move. She got married right out of Toplofty.

To money. To a Siwash man, as a matter of fact.

As if to show Dad that she could beat him at his own crazy game. And then, not at all incidentally, it prevented her from having to come home again after her graduation.

But three days before the wedding, the groom's father had a heart attack.

It didn't kill him. But the groom and his mother took it very seriously. They insisted that the wedding was off. The marriage could proceed, but the big wedding would have to be canceled.

It was what my parents had been looking forward to.

Sis was their only daughter, after all. All their friends, all
Dad's clients, all our relatives had been invited. And had
accepted. Gifts had started to arrive. It was too late to get a
refund from the caterer or the florist, although I really don't
think that was uppermost in their minds.

What I think they had in mind was a picture of how it
was all supposed to be. Mother, Dad, Bride, Groom,
Groom's Parents.

Okay, so he'd had a heart attack. But he was stable. He
was holding on. My father suggested that they hold the
wedding as planned and that the kids then go to the groom's
father's hospital room with the rabbi and that they go
through the ceremony again there. But the groom's mother
wouldn't hear of it. She insisted that the big wedding was
"inappropriate" and that the children be married in the
apartment, in the bedroom where the groom's father was
convalescing.

He was already out of the hospital, already home?

Yes, but with nurses round the clock!

"No wedding, no marriage," my father declared.

But Sis betrayed him. That was Dad's word for what
she did. And he didn't talk to her for the next eleven years.

She had a miscarriage, and then two daughters, and
then, eleven years after that wedding in the bedroom of the
groom's convalescent father, she and he were divorced.

Then Dad talked to her again.

During those years, Mom would sometimes sneak off to
visit her. I must confess that her husband and I didn't hit it
off very well. He was a pompous little guy with thick
glasses—which he couldn't help—and a condescending
know-it-all attitude for which he could be held responsible.
He didn't exactly drive me crazy, but he managed to make
me very cranky. Whatever it was about wines, food, plays,
books, cars, stereo equipment, ski slopes, opera recordings,

he knew it, owned it, had a better one, had bought it cheaper, or had bought the last one before they fell apart and started to turn out shoddy goods. He was insufferable!

But he was never the real issue. The truth of the matter is that Sis had never forgiven me for those tickling sessions. Or for having been the unwilling star of the dinner table. Or for having gone to Siwash when she couldn't.

She just loved it when her husband put me down.

I didn't love it. I lost my temper and told her I thought that Dad had been right and that she'd made a terrible mistake.

So we didn't talk, either, for almost eleven years.

When Dad died, we both came home for the funeral.

We'd been on speaking terms since her divorce, as if nothing had happened, as if we were the kids in the photograph on our parents' dresser, only older but still looking at each other with affection. A posed picture, of course. But even such icons have their power, and we would call back and forth every week or so. We did this for some years.

It was not altogether a surprise, though, that at the end of that week of the funeral there should have been some rupture, some quarrel to mar the ritual enactment of our grief and loss. It was just a matter of waiting to see when it would come, and how, and how bad it would be. I don't remember now exactly what triggered it. We were talking about something Dad had said or done, or maybe something we had remembered from our childhood days in that house. I think I corrected something she said. I remembered it differently, at any rate, and said so. What she thought was red, I remembered as green. What she was sure had happened in November, I recalled quite vividly as having happened in May. Something dumb like that and unimportant.

But it was important to her, or being corrected was. Or being corrected by me was.

"Don't contradict me. Nobody died and left you king!" she said.

"What a grotesque thing to say!" I said, as much amused by the locution as actually shocked.

But that was enough to call forth all the venom, all the rage and hurt that had been festering there for years. She had been working with some sort of psychotherapist, I think as a result of her divorce, and they had no doubt touched on her relationship with Dad. (It would have been crazy if they had not done so.)

She was just getting to the point where she was learning to express her anger. And there she was, silenced by Dad's death. It does no good to express anger to a corpse. She'd been cut out again.

But I was there and available, and the next best thing. So she let me have it, twenty minutes of scatology and anguish, which is a long stint. Try it sometime.

I did what I remembered having done as a little boy when Dad yelled at me: I concentrated on not smiling, trying not to think about how well he could perform these rhetorical turns and cadences, trying to keep from grinning like a clown as I was so sorely tempted to do.

I understood what she was doing. I could even feel a degree of sympathy for her. On the other hand, it was painful for Mom to hear. She had this picture in her head of how the family was now supposed to be—herself, the widow, and her two bereaved children, and the solemn grandchildren seated around the living room, talking in low tones.

Mother, Son, Daughter, and Grandchildren. In decorous mourning. But there was a certain sense to what Sis was saying, I guess, what she was wailing about and inveighing against. She, too, had loved our father. She had wanted his love—and in simple justice should have had more of it, more attention, more affection, than she'd ever received. She had always been in the background, and I had always been the star. But now the production was over. Dead and gone!

Okay, okay. But in fairness, I hadn't volunteered for my role. I wasn't the one she was angry at and couldn't argue with anymore.

What was there to do but sit and listen? I sat and listened.

Eventually she subsided, just got tired and stopped.

It would have been nice if she'd apologized, but she didn't. I guess I never really expected her to.

I excused myself and went for a walk around the old neighborhood, feeling like a stranger, an impostor. This wasn't how things were supposed to be.

But, as I say, the trick may be not to pay too close attention, to see things with your eyes closed.

I went back to the house, and somehow we managed to get through the rest of the afternoon without further insult.

She was annoyed. But I was annoyed now, too, although not seriously angry. I figured she'd calm down after a bit and realize that she'd behaved badly. I figured that in a day or two she might call me to say she was sorry. When that didn't happen, I suppose I adjusted to the idea that she'd let a week go by and then call, without apologizing, as if nothing had ever happened. Or as if our groans of bereavement were loud enough to drown out any minor dissonances.

Some such gambit would have worked and could have allowed us at least to continue the way we were supposed to: brother and sister, not quite the way we looked in that odd, old-fashioned sepia photograph on our parents' bedroom dresser, but close enough, still talking to each other, anyway.

But nothing. Not a word. And it occurred to me that she was not going to call, that if anybody was going to make

the call, it would have to be me. I waited a few months—
all right, almost a year—until there was an appropriate occasion, an excuse, and when my daughter gave birth to a
daughter, I called Sis right away to announce the good
news. She congratulated me but said she was on her way
out the door.

"Talk to you soon," I said, prompting. It was her turn
now.

It still is.

So I am standing in for Dad again, but this time as the
victim of the silence rather than as its instigator. She feels
perfectly justified, righteous in the anger she has directed at
me, not for what I said or how I'd corrected her recollection
of whatever it was—I swear I can't even remember—but
for the attention I got all those years, at all those dinners
when we were kids. Or maybe for my tickling her so hard
and then preventing her from calling Mom and Dad.

I think of her every now and then. I'm sure she thinks
of me every once in a while, too. But each time the decision
each of us makes is not to pick up the phone.

Stupid, but there it is. And likely to continue. It is as
if we were punishing each other, as if we were each being
punished for something. And punishment gets to be a habit,
a way of life, or at least something to hold onto. I can't help
thinking that, on my side as well as on hers, it may even be
deserved.

Parents' Day

It ought to have been a great occasion, one of life's significant milestones. But there's the catch, Saul realized. You expect those big moments to be pleasurable, proud, and happy times that prove you have lived your life correctly. And if not? If you've screwed up or, to be charitable, have just been unlucky? Then those great occasions turn into indictments, judgments, and punishments all at once.

From such self-inflicted torments have theologians devised ideas of hell. Even the car Saul was driving, a nine-year-old station wagon whose exterior he had deliberately allowed to deteriorate in order to discourage adolescent car thieves, was a true mark against him. There would be Volvos and Saabs and Mercedes and BMWs lined up in the parking lot behind Hamilton Hall, making their smug statements about their owners' successes. This old heap might, if someone else was driving it, proclaim a lofty indifference to worldly concerns. But to be persuasive, that somebody else would have to be able to afford better and choose not to. What with Saul's alimony payments and Abel's tuition bills, he could barely afford the insurance premiums and repair bills on this shabby wagon.

He had considered renting a car for the day, just to have something less disgraceful in which to arrive and depart, but that had seemed unacceptable, too, cowardly and fake. Besides, the odds were that he wouldn't recognize anyone—or be recognized, either, which was more to the point. This wasn't a class reunion, after all, but Parents' Day. Saul's great achievement, which nobody could take away from him, was in having fathered Abel, a bright, sensitive kid. And Abel was now a student here at Saul's old school.

Saul's own life was hardly relevant on a day like this. What was important was the youngster to whom he was only too willing to yield the rigors and comforts of the school's regimen in its Georgian buildings so grandly disposed in inevitable quadrangles. Saul nevertheless had devoted considerable thought to his personal appearance, deciding at last on his navy blue blazer and gray flannel trousers. He would dress down rather than up, but neatly. Like a Horatio Alger hero, poor but honest, threadbare but clean.

Actually, he'd been thinking more of Tony Randall, who had pronounced on some talk show not long before that he never wore anything but a blazer and flannels. Here at the school the kids looked as though they'd chosen their clothing more or less at random from Goodwill bins and L. L. Bean catalogs. The boys, required to wear neckties, sported as often as not gaudy creations they thought were funny—old-fashioned wide ties they had retrieved from the backs of their fathers' closets. Saul wore a perfectly correct silk-rep Brooks Brothers tie he had bought at Filene's basement.

He parked without incident or encounter and, from habit, locked the car. He walked around to the front entrance of Hamilton Hall, and it all came back to him, that array of coat hooks in the outer vestibule and the distinctive odor of the building, partly from the furniture polish they used, evidently the same brand as thirty years before. And the scale of the place. Or did it seem smaller now than what he thought he remembered?

There were tables at which the parents were to pick up

their information packets, which were arranged alphabetically, and there were students sitting behind each of the tables prepared, presumably, to help those parents who could not read their own names. The thought brought some comfort to Saul, not because it was so clever, but because it was recognizably his own, the same kind of wiseass comment he'd fashioned when he was a kid here and wiseass comments were the only way to fight back against the domineering power the school could bring to bear on its students. Usually the school had the parents squarely behind it, too—people who had to believe in what the school was doing, or else they wouldn't have been paying the large tuitions and room-and-board charges. Or parents who, like Saul, had no choice and hoped that a boarding school could be a neutral ground in the battlefields of divorce.

The tuitions were larger now, even allowing for inflation. But it had been a matter of pride for Saul to do for his child what had been done for him, to repay his own parents the only way he knew how. And if Abel found it burdensome to be the beneficiary of this arrangement, that was okay. To tell the truth, Saul liked the school more in retrospect than when he'd been part of it. To come back like this as a parent was, he told himself once more, a good thing.

Without help, he found his packet and then walked over to one of the tables on the opposite wall where there were coffee urns and trays of doughnuts. He passed up the doughnuts, not wanting to risk getting the powdered sugar all over his blazer, but he took a polystyrene cup and filled it with coffee. He carried it into the auditorium. The huge brass chandelier still gleamed. The white walls still seemed to soar. It had been designed as an impressive, inspiring room, and it worked. The old Congregational virtues and defects were here together: not only the belief in hard work but also the sure conviction that appropriate rewards would be equitably and immediately forthcoming.

But what else was there to teach kids? All that stuff about moral education always sounded great, but nobody ever specified which morality, what values, whose philosophy—as if it were rude even to raise such questions. They got raised anyway, as Saul knew perfectly well, in bull sessions in the kids' rooms. Or in therapy sessions in the offices of their psychiatrists. Or later on, in what was condescendingly referred to as "life."

Saul realized he was glad to be subject no longer to the school's power, could no longer be forced to go five times a week to chapel services, which were nondenominational school assemblies flavored with a couple of hymns and punctuated at the end by an organ recessional, usually something from Bach. The headmaster's eyes had glared out from just above the lectern, and he had looked wise and powerful in the academic robes he wore in the English style. But the pieties he'd spouted about responsibility and effort and idealism had rung hollow, even then. The boys knew perfectly well that it was another attempt to get them not only to obey but to swallow and digest the school rule book.

Still, what had been the choices? The public schools in most large cities were ineffective, if not actually dangerous. And it was truer now. The school could be as corrupt and as pompous as it liked, as long as its reputation held and it continued to receive ten applicants for each available place. With good students, bright kids from ambitious families, it was tough to screw up. It happened even so, but the school rid itself of its problems by expelling kids who got into trouble, which public schools couldn't do.

Carrying his coffee carefully, Saul made his way to an empty seat in the back row of the already crowded auditorium. The coffee, he discovered, was terrible. And because the floor was raked toward the platform at the front of the room, there was no way just to put the cup down under the seat. It would almost certainly spill. Saul didn't feel like working his way back to the aisle and returning to the lobby. His only other choice was to hold the nasty stuff until the end of the opening address.

The headmaster, the dean of students, and a couple of other faculty members came marching in, not wearing their robes this time—was it because they did not dare such pomposity before the parents? They filed onto the stage and took their seats. The headmaster came to the lectern to welcome the parents and to answer what he was sure was their first question: Where were their kids?

The answer was that the whole school had been mobilized for the day to police the grounds, to pitch in and clean up the athletic fields and the bird sanctuary and the Great Quad, to pick up leaves and waste paper and discarded candy wrappers and soda bottles, and make the place decent. The parents, meanwhile, would be going to the classes from which their youngsters had been excused. "In the packets you picked up on your way in, you'll find your schedules with the class listings, followed by the names of your teachers and the names of the buildings and the room numbers. These will be abbreviated sessions, twenty-five minutes instead of the usual fifty-minute classes, but there should be time enough for you to get a sense of what the classes are like, and even for some of you to chat with the teachers if you wish, or if they think there's some special need."

In a way it all sounded perfectly reasonable. People around Saul were nodding and even smiling. But for Saul it was a kind of nightmare, to be thrust back in time this way, arbitrarily and without warning, and to be made to go through the old drill again. It was like the business of the coffee cup, some perfectly innocent and insignificant gesture that turns around and grows into a medium-to-large awkwardness.

Abel and the other youngsters were out doing the work

of the groundskeepers—menials without pay—in the name of "character building." Meanwhile Saul and the other parents were to be hustled through a sample day of sitting in classrooms, of having to raise their hands to speak or to ask leave to go to the bathroom. Why were the people around him smiling? Obviously they weren't alumni. Or alumnae . . . The women were too old, anyway; the school had gone co-ed only a decade or so ago.

He told himself he was being silly. There was nothing ominous in any of this. He already had his diploma, for God's sake, and they could not take it away. On the other hand, to be subjected again to the constraints of the academy wasn't any cause for celebration.

It occurred to him suddenly that Abel was hardly likely to be any more enthusiastic than he was about the school's demands and his subjection to its rules and dictates. But that's what kids have to put up with, Saul argued, calming himself as he had often done before by formulating the problem in a less ominous way. The idea of childhood being such a terrific time is romantic and maybe peculiarly American. The British and French have no such sentimental illusions. To them, childhood is an uncomfortable time that you wait out in order to reach adulthood with its privileges and comforts.

As he left the auditorium, Saul was able to throw his coffee cup into one of the large receptacles that had been put out for the occasion. Relieved of that burden, he also managed to shrug off the other baggage, his suspicion of the school's motives. Why not go through a sample day, sitting in Abel's classrooms and looking at the faces Abel had to look at every day? It could be interesting. It might even be fun. He consulted the schedule in his information packet. Latin, History, English, Math, and Biology.

The Latin had been Saul's idea. Abel had accepted his father's claim that it was actually easier than either French

or German, which required an ear. In Latin, there was no
need to speak the language and hardly much occasion to
write in it. You had only to read it, and if you were willing
to learn the vocabulary, it was pretty straightforward.

All true enough, but Saul was nonetheless pleased at
the idea that Abel was going every morning to old Farnam
Hall to sit in one of those bare rooms with the busts of
Cicero and Virgil and Ovid and Plautus staring down from
the niches between the tall windows and to go through the
inevitable calculations he could still remember: looking to
see whom the teacher had called on first, counting out the
number of intervening bodies and the number of intervening sentences, and then trying to figure out ahead of time
the correct translation of the sentence that would be his. The
smell of chalk dust still hung in the air, mixed with the
nervous sweat of those who were relying more on that
counting system than on their preparations of the previous
night.

Saul had a veteran's pride in having come through it.
On the other hand, he knew that social psychologists would
refer to dissonance theory to explain this after-the-fact approval, saying that the experience itself had been so disagreeable as to require him to be proud of it and profess to
have loved it—because the alternative was to admit that he
had been miserable, had been a fool to put up with it at the
time, and had cause to blame rather than thank his parents
for having sent him here. What did they know? They had
bought the reputation of the place, its great age, the altogether irrelevant fact that some nephew of George Washington had once come to school here (although he'd never been
heard of again, living as obscurely as many of the children
of privilege who had followed him through these hallowed
halls and then disappeared).

Around him, parents were seating themselves in the
peculiar varnished oak chairs with the one arm that broad-

ened out to form a writing surface. Men and women his age, they looked comfortable, assured, cheerful. That was another indictment, Saul decided, more serious than the one he'd survived in the parking lot, because he wasn't any of those things—and he'd gone to school here. But that counted less, somehow, than the lush tweeds and soft cashmeres of the couple to his right, for example. Their ability to float through the world approvingly was what he envied. That and, of course, the fact that they were still married, that their kid came home or joined them in their condo in Montego Bay or their chalet in Cortina d'Ampezzo.

It was what he'd done twenty years ago, idealizing the lives of his classmates and then comparing himself and finding himself inadequate. Dopey, but that was what the school itself encouraged. Deliberately competitive, it even published the class standings of each of the students in a list on the wall of Hamilton Hall and included the news in the reports it sent home—that you were 48th, say, in a class of 166. That, too, they called "character building."

The teacher appeared at the front of the room, a Mr. Hancock, whose youth made Saul smile. Obviously this was not one of the masters, but some student, some nervy kid who had put on a sport coat and was about to impersonate a particularly detestable teacher in a grand prank. But it wasn't a prank. This really was Hancock, a youngster in his early twenties, maybe, fresh out of Harvard or Yale, with a job teaching Latin here, and coaching club soccer probably. And lucky to get it, too. He wrote his name on the board, greeted the parents, and started talking to them about the relevance and usefulness of Latin, not only as a vocabulary builder but as an exercise in orderly thinking.

Saul didn't like it. He didn't like Mr. Hancock, and he resented his spiel. There didn't need to be any extrinsic justification for the teaching of Latin. It was, like virtue, its own reward.

"How many of you have ever studied Latin?" Mr. Hancock asked at one point.

A few hands went up, Saul's not among them. He had not been sworn, and his background was nobody's business. That he'd been here in this building studying Latin under Mr. Colby and Mr. Benton was his own affair. Both of them were dead now, anyway.

Saul supposed that if somehow he were caught out, he could justify himself, saying he hadn't wanted to embarrass any of the parents who had never taken Latin. The truth was less charming: that he'd learned, in this building, in this very room, never to raise his hand, never to volunteer. As in the army. As in a lot of situations one comes up against later on in "life."

Mr. Hancock was explaining for those who had never bothered to examine the school's catalog what the classics offerings were and how the program allowed the greatest possible flexibility so that students transferring from other schools could find their right level and their right speed here and then make as much progress as possible. There were intensive classes and remedial classes and also the standard sequence of courses in both Latin and Greek. But even those courses were improved now. In Latin, for instance, instead of the usual menu of Caesar, Cicero, and Virgil, there was more variety, an emphasis on comparative linguistics, and an attempt at opening up the windows to let some fresh air into the old stuffiness.

Saul remembered that stuffiness and supposed he approved. There was a lot to be said for replacing those thickets of Ciceronian syntax with almost anything else.

A bell clanged in the hall outside the classroom, startling Saul and the other parents, too. He'd forgotten the bells. Like bells in prisons.

Mr. Hancock wanted parents of the following to stay for a few moments if they could manage that, and he read out a short list of last names, including, of course, Saul's.

Abel's, but Saul's, too.

Saul's first.

As if he'd screwed up the count and worked out the wrong sentence.

"Are those parents here?" Hancock asked. Slowly, Saul raised his hand. It was meanspirited of him to note with satisfaction that the tweed-and-cashmere couple had to raise their hands as well.

It turned out, though, that their little girl was working hard to catch up after a long bout in the infirmary, and Mr. Hancock just wanted to let them know how well she'd been doing.

Abel's situation was less cheerful. He was a bright youngster, Mr. Hancock assured Saul, but he lacked discipline. It was mostly weakness in vocabulary. If he would spend a little more time and effort drilling himself, perhaps with another student . . .

"I thought you said it was different now, that there was more emphasis on linguistics, and that you'd opened the windows," Saul said, defensively. And then, knowing it wasn't such a good idea, he looked around and said, "The windows look pretty much the way they always did."

Hancock was quick enough with his reply. "In any study of a foreign language, there's a certain amount of brute work, just plain unglamorous memorization," he said. And then, "But I didn't see your hand."

"My hand?"

"When I asked who had studied Latin."

"I didn't like being put on the spot that way," Saul said. "Or having the others put on the spot."

"And where was it that you studied Latin?"

"Right here in this room," Saul said. "I didn't like being put on the spot then, either."

"Perhaps it's an attitude problem, then," Mr. Hancock suggested. "Abel's, I mean. I think you ought to have a talk with him. He's in danger of failing, which is not going to do much good in the way of settling old scores or whatever you and he are trying to do. Either you know this stuff or you don't. It's that simple. It doesn't take a lot of talent. Just hard work. He's got to learn the words. And he's got to get his butt out of bed and come to class in the morning."

"I'll talk to him," Saul said.

"That may help," Mr. Hancock replied, obviously without much conviction, and then he turned to the third father, who was waiting to hear about his kid, wondering whether it would be encouraging news or this other, sadder routine. Saul knew he was dismissed. He didn't hang around to hear about the third kid.

Having waited to talk to Mr. Hancock, though, he was late for history and had to hurry. Or, no, he told himself, he didn't have to do anything anymore. He was a grown-up and no longer at their mercy. Never again would he have to calculate worriedly whether the train was late coming into Boston, whether he could make up enough of the lost time by taking a cab from Back Bay to North Station so he could catch that last train, which would get him into his dorm in time to avoid a demerit. No more of that stupid business! Still, for a person who had nothing to worry about, he was walking very rapidly. And when he arrived at last, Mr. Peabody pounced on him as if he were any other student, either to show off a little or just out of habit. Peabody stopped talking and stood there in the front of the room, leaning against the desk in a stagy exaggeration of patience, his arms folded, his head cocked to one side, as he waited for Saul to seat himself in the back.

"And what have you to say for yourself, then?" he asked, when Saul had finally found a chair.

Saul could hardly believe it. "I was detained. I'm sorry," he managed.

"Very well, I'll begin again," Mr. Peabody said, biting his consonants.

Peabody was an older man, one of the few who had actually been a member of the faculty, albeit a junior member, back when Saul was a student. Saul had never been in any of Mr. Peabody's classes, and at the moment this did not seem to be much cause for regret. Indeed, it was interesting to see what had become of the man, to learn how these years at the academy had turned him into a bully and, unless there was some exotic medical problem to explain the capillaries around the nose, something of a drunk, too.

Without much conviction, indeed with some scintillating charge of irony as if he didn't quite believe what he was saying or didn't think his listeners were getting the joke of it, he explained how the course was set up not only to teach the history of the United States but also to help the students learn how to organize material, how to create their own textbooks from original sources and primary materials, how to use the resources from which historians must smelt and refine "in a mysterious process we call historiography."

He spoke as if he were too good for this, as if he were holding back, just out of good manners, the obvious remark that very few of his students were likely to go on to do any serious work as historians, or historiographers. Or was Saul being paranoid again?

It was no surprise at the end of Mr. Peabody's presentation for Saul to hear his name called out. He knew what the problem was: an exam that Abel had missed. He'd been ill but had not gone to the infirmary, and therefore he didn't have a medical excuse. As Abel had already explained to Saul, he'd wanted to take the exam and had planned to go to the infirmary immediately after the test, but instead he'd felt terrible, had gone to his room to lie down for twenty minutes or so in the period before his history class, and had fallen asleep.

Saul believed him. But there was no proof. And there was no particular point in trying to convince this cynical old fart, who would dismiss anything Saul said as the foolish testimony of a fond parent who either had been bamboozled himself or was just trying to make things better for his kid.

If Peabody hadn't already done what he could to humiliate him for having come into class a few moments late, Saul might have decided the other way. But this extra information, hardly irrelevant, was new evidence either for a would-be historiographer or even for a mere actor on history's stage. When he heard his name called, there was hardly any question as to what he would do. He just pretended to be deaf, to be absent, to be an alien from another planet who had to get back to his spacecraft. Without looking back, he walked out with the other parents, out of the room, out of the building, and across the tidy quadrangle the students had so carefully policed.

This was not what he'd expected to be doing on Parents' Day. This was what Elaine might have predicted, though. Fortunately she would not be likely to have the satisfaction of knowing, at least this once, that her mean expectations had been justified and accurate. Saul strolled over toward Holmes Hall almost serenely, as if he had triumphed, as if he and Abel had shared a victory together in Peabody's class.

Abel's English teacher was a Ms. Norman. There were women on the faculty now, and forty percent of the students were girls, which was probably a good thing, Saul thought. Ms. Norman, though, was perhaps excessive in her attempts to draw out the students from what she called the dry and dull exercises of ingestion and regurgitation of information. She wanted, instead, to put them in touch with their feelings and help them use their personalities in the creation of a personal style.

Not a contemptible ambition, by any means, but it was a tall order for adolescents. She was the one teacher to whom Saul hoped to talk for a few minutes, if only to explain that some of Abel's reticence about personal details might have arisen from the fact that his parents had recently divorced. Saul felt sure there were other students in this awkward predicament. Ms. Norman, a young woman just starting out, would be easier to talk to than an old veteran like Peabody. Saul was able to invent almost instantly a plausible story for this slender, not quite mousy woman who stood before them, a bookish girl who hadn't quite the assertiveness to go on to college teaching. Or, no, give her more credit and say that she preferred students in secondary school, students whom she could still help mold.

She talked more or less sensibly about the academy's English program, the absolute requirement for a certain level of competence in written and spoken expression, and the collateral requirement that students be able to understand texts of a certain degree of complexity. Her own emphasis, she added, was on getting the young men and women to understand language and literature as avenues of emotional expression and understanding—which made for better communication and also better humanity. The students resisted this, she admitted cheerfully, because they were young and shy. But she felt close enough to them to think she could give them a certain confidence and let them know that their feelings mattered.

Saul surprised himself, raising his hand.

"Yes?" Ms. Norman asked.

"Isn't it possible that their feelings matter too much to be used as classroom exercises?" he asked. "Don't they have a certain right to emotional privacy?"

She glared at him as if he were a troublemaker, one of

those obstreperous youngsters who was resisting her out of pure contrariness. "Language is an intimate, emotional business," she said. "Education is an intimate and emotional undertaking. The students are here because their parents trust us. You do trust us, don't you? If you didn't, I wouldn't expect you to send your youngsters off to such a place but to keep them at home."

He was tempted to argue but didn't want to take up class time. He realized it would take longer than he'd first supposed. He'd have to work out a way of raising the question in such a way that it would not be a challenge to her, would not be offensive to her touchy sense of her own importance in this job. Jesus! The obverse of Peabody, but just as bad. Worse even, because she supposed she was doing her students good. Confronted in the dead of night and with a gun held to his head, Peabody would be likely to admit that he had long ago abandoned any such fantasies.

Saul caught himself. He had been squirming in his seat like a resentful student who cannot see any use in these sacrifices and restrictions. He concentrated on sitting up straight and looking just above Ms. Norman's head, which was a trick he remembered from the old days. It made one appear to be concentrating on every damned syllable as it fell like a simulated pearl from the mouth of a swine . . .

Don't smile! He leaned his elbow on the writing surface of the chair arm and buried his chin and his mouth in his palm the way he had done years before. And he concentrated on not grinning. Think of something sad! He thought of Abel, enduring these assaults but with no prospect of driving away later in the day, with years of this stretching out in front of him as they must appear to be doing to a youngster of that age for whom time goes so slowly.

At least when Abel and the school disagreed, Saul sided with Abel. His own parents had always assumed that the school was right, that he ought to buckle down and work harder, be more serious, get better grades and fewer demerits, and make it into a good university as they had never had the chance to do.

He couldn't blame them. But Abel could blame him, who should have known better, who ought to have understood what horses' asses these people were but had nonetheless committed his child to their care. How could he have done such a thing?

Ms. Norman had dismissed the class, the mock class, the miniclass. Saul waited behind, as it was his right to do. He was a parent, after all, a customer. As the headmaster had announced earlier in the morning, she was here to answer his questions. Saul waited for her to finish talking with another couple whose child, imaginative enough and even gifted, was still having problems with proofreading, so that her grades did not reflect her considerable abilities.

Ms. Norman, it seemed, was willing to sacrifice a little of that creativity and imagination for the sake of orderliness and accuracy. It would be the world's standard, she said—rather smugly, Saul thought—and the girl had better learn to accommodate herself to it. There was something to be said for old Peabody, Saul thought. He demanded the same kinds of accuracy and conformity, no doubt, but without any of this idealistic bullshit.

When the other parents had left, Saul introduced himself and apologized for having interrupted her presentation. Still, he was a little troubled by her approach, and he asked whether she had had any training in adolescent psychology. Was she aware that some of these kids might be going through difficult times and that her expectations—that they draw on their inner emotional lives and use the details of their private and family experience for classwork—might be burdensome to some of them?

"You are referring, I suppose, to the fact that you and Abel's mother are divorcing?"

"Well, yes," he said. "I think it's tough on Abel. I think it would be tough on any child in that circumstance."

"The assumption here is that students are healthy and well adjusted, on the playing field and in the classroom. If we were to cater to every claim of disability, nobody would do anything or learn anything."

"I don't see how theorems in geometry or conjugations in Latin would be affected," Saul said, reasonably enough, he thought.

"English is a requirement."

"Amateur psychotherapy is not," Saul protested.

"If you're dissatisfied, perhaps you should speak with the headmaster. This school has a certain tradition—"

"I went to this school!" Saul insisted.

She didn't answer. She just stared at him.

"Thank you for your time," he said. It was what he had learned long ago to say to people with whom he was getting nowhere.

"What we need," she said as soon as he had turned away, "is your support rather than your resistance. What Abel needs, that is."

He didn't answer. He didn't need advice about what his son required of him. Or, to be more precise, what prompting he might have needed he had already received in abundance. He was neck-deep in it.

Outside he checked his watch. He was ten minutes late for math. Cut math. Or, as Abel would say, bag it. Abel was doing okay in math, anyway, claiming a B, which might be a B − or even a C + but could perhaps be a legitimate B. Still, considering his problems in other courses, math was not a cause of any particular concern. Biology in twenty-five minutes then?

He supposed he ought to show up.

But he had a little time. He could walk around the campus a little, looking for something soothing, something recognizable, something small and private that had given him pleasure or had spoken to him years before. There had to be some trick of the light, perhaps as the sun glinted off the windowpanes of the old buildings. Or, if not that, then something like it.

What he had learned here, he realized, and what he reached for now was the art of getting through the next little chunk of time, the trick of climbing out of himself and becoming his own analyst, becoming in any event his own observer, checking his psyche's dials and meters and trying to dope out the prognosis for the next few minutes.

That was one of the things Elaine had found so infuriating. But it was the only way he had ever learned to cope with unreasonable and often unfriendly demands.

The trees were in bud, and they showed a delicate shade of green that would darken and coarsen in the next week or so. It was a pretty school, huge amounts of money having been donated by a few alumni for the purposes of landscaping and external beautification. Some of the old buildings had been jacked up and carted around into more pleasing configurations—that had happened several years before Saul's time. But the prettiness of the place was not soothing. It had, in fact, always seemed a kind of mockery, like elaborate plantings of flowers around a mental hospital or a prison. With the inmates doing the maintenance work.

As here, as now.

And, as always, in the name of character and discipline.

He had been walking faster and faster. And he remembered a dumb thing he had done once. He hadn't forgotten it so much as put it away, suppressing it because it was so dismal. But he remembered it now. It was an odd thing for him to have done then, because he hadn't been a jock. He had barely been able to make the sandpit in the broad jump, the event he'd chosen in the winter term of his senior year in Social Track—the elective nonathletes picked because it wasn't very demanding.

He hadn't done this for any requirement, though. This had been his own idea, his own project entirely. And thinking about it now, he started to jog past the belltower toward the hockey rink and beyond that to the old gym, the one that in his time had been the only gym. Inside, on the second floor, there was a wooden track around which one could run, making a wonderful thundering noise.

Just one lap, he promised himself.

If there was something going on, of course, he could excuse himself and go away. But he knew the building would probably be empty. The faculty were in their classrooms. The students were out there, organized into squads he had seen hunting for candy wrappers.

Nobody was there. He took off his shoes and socks because there used to be a rule against running in street shoes, either for safety or to preserve the track. Just one time around. To feel the beginnings of the pain. That was what he remembered, that pain in his chest, the burning in his lungs from sudden exertion, a pain that was not hostile or frightening because he could control it, because it was a part of him that was his own, having nothing to do with the school or with his parents, or with their unrealistic views of it and him.

He wondered whether Abel had devised any such escape mechanism. He wondered why Abel should have to! Saul knew he had made a terrible mistake, had sent Abel here out of pride and because it was convenient and to get him away from Elaine. But it had been wrong, and the boy was suffering for it. If he had any decency, if he had learned anything at this damnable place, it would be to free his son from its clutches. To take him home and let him do as he pleased. At least to let him decide what he wanted to do.

Saul finished his lap but could not stop. He knew that there was a higher level of pain at which he would be excused from thinking, at which his body's distress would drive away the other distresses that came from his mind. He could feel the sting of each footfall and the promise of a burning beyond which was oblivion, something close to what a drunk must find in the bottle. Or a dope addict with the needle. A small discomfort and then a large release.

The sound was soothing, a boom-boom that echoed in the huge empty space and resonated among the beams and steel poles by which the track hung from the old girdered ceiling. He was going well now. He wasn't a jogger or a runner and he had a terrible style, but that didn't matter. He was running, not for speed or to get anywhere, but for the pain itself.

Pain to make up for the boy's pain, for his son's hurt and rage at parents who had destroyed his family and his world. And at the school for bothering him, for picking at him—as Saul knew that Mr. Peabody and Ms. Norman and Mr. Hancock did every day, all the while supposing that they were doing right and proper things.

There were tears now, partly of pain and partly of grief. If only he could let the boy know how sorry he was, or could let these tears be all for Abel. He would have been willing to keep on running, to run forever, to run until he dropped.

But he didn't. He knew that wouldn't be helping Abel at all. Instead he stopped and went outside to wait for the sweat to dry. He found a bathroom where he could wash his face, blot himself dry with paper towels, and straighten his hair a little with his fingers.

And then he was ready to meet Abel for the lunch that the schedule had listed for the next chunk of time. He'd cut math and biology and felt guilty about it. About that, too, he was ashamed of himself.

But if his kid was brave enough to come to this parents' lunch with him, he could be brave, too, and do his part. Or braver—though Saul had no way to measure how much—because he knew he had greater cause for shame.

Instructions

1. Never wear a brown hat with a blue suit.

2. Don't forget to floss every day. Brush every morning and every night. Don't mix grape and grain. Don't try to use a fork to eat olives. Never bet on a gray horse.

3. Always remember your parents' birthdays. It isn't the gift that counts but the thought. It is better to give than to receive. I before E, except after C, or when sounded like A, as in Neighbor or Weigh. (But what about Seize?)

4. Never wear a bow tie with a button-down collar. Why not? Because! Because you don't, that's why. Because I say so! Would I tell you something that isn't true? Think of what I've done for you, of the sacrifices we've made for you. And what do we ask in return? What? Nothing at all, except that you take full advantage! We want what's best for you. And that you don't open up a mouth! A fresh-mouthed kid who always thinks he knows it all . . .

5. Change your underwear every day, and never wear underwear with holes in it. You'll be ashamed in the emergency room, where they'll take you after you've been run over by a bus, when they see what a slob you are.

6. It follows from the foregoing that if you wear clean underwear without holes, you will not be run over by a bus—which is okay. In the same way it happened with those sentences when you were properly prepared and were ready to translate and you were never called on. Think about it.

7. Listen, these things are telling you something that's true! In a world as confusing as ours, that's a claim that carries a lot of majesty—and also arouses a lot of suspicions. Or if it doesn't, it ought to. It does in me, anyway. Truth? What is that? Immediately I see Jehovah's Witnesses standing on my porch with their pathetic hats with plastic cherries on the brim and their smiles of goodwill. And fat! Aren't there any thin Jehovah's Witnesses? Are they trying to make up in weight what they lack in numbers? I'm as cynical as the next fellow, maybe even more so—especially if the next fellow is a Jehovah's Witness. I think truth is mostly to be found in labeling. This product contains no sodium! You can believe in that, can't you? And in instructions. Who can argue with a numbered paragraph that demands of you nothing more than that you insert Tab A into Slot B and glue?

8. Ignore this sentence.

9. What an absurd, what a perfectly useless piece of instruction! I'm being the smart-ass author, screwing around and playing games. But you are wise to me already, aren't you? It's not as if you could have prepared yourself in any way. Those three words ganged up on you, and by the time you had taken them in, they'd taken you in, announcing that you had wasted your time, that you'd been had. It isn't as if I'd written, "Skip the next paragraph."

10. Skip the next paragraph. (You saw that coming, didn't you?)

11. Okay, okay. But now what's your excuse? Or what's mine? For you begin to resent this or, just as dangerous for this fragile relationship of ours, you begin to tire of it. You are starting to think about dropping the entire thing, turning the page, or putting away this book for another more promising one. You come to these encounters expecting to be charmed. And you're entitled. After all, it's your time, your money, your life. You can invite whomever you like.

Or disinvite. There's no particular need to persist in this. You've had fair warning, after all, and whom else can you blame if you persist in this foolish course? You knew what you were getting into, didn't you, but you just wouldn't listen. You were never an easy person to talk to, never an easy person to advise, even when you knew we had your best interests at heart. You are not following instructions. Or using time and materials well. You call yourself a divergent thinker, but what does that mean, what does that amount to, Mr. High-and-Mighty, except classroom clown? Or pest? Who are you to give yourself such airs?

12. Don't give yourself airs. Take it from me, you'll be doing yourself an infinite amount of harm. What kind of life do you think you can expect for yourself? Your parents were right, after all. As parents usually are, even though children never understand this. Your parents meant well and had learned a thing or two in their time. And what did they do to you that was so terrible? They did what they did, perhaps repressing the blossoming of your best and truest self, but they quite honestly believed what they said—or shouted—when they told you how they were "doing this for your own good, and the day will come, mark my words, when you'll thank me."

13. Ignore the previous paragraph.

14. Be trustworthy, loyal, helpful, friendly, courteous, kind, obedient, cheerful, thrifty, brave, clean, and reverent. Be prepared.

15. Forget step 13.

16. Skip it. I did. I learned over the years how to listen and not listen, how to turn off the actual meaning and attend only to the rise and fall of the inflections, as if the yelling were in some other language. The rise and fall of the voice, the rhetorical tropes and operatic turns that were expressive not only of anger but also of an irrelevant aesthetic predilection for balance and shapeliness. The parallelisms, the set-ups and payoffs, the antiphonal arrangements of rhetorical

questions and emotive answers. These waves of language would break over my head, pounding at me like the surf of a storm-lashed sea.

17. Don't laugh. It's ruinous to laugh, even to smile, even when they get off a terrific line, something new that you haven't heard before, some razzle-dazzle bit of business that has just revealed itself to one of them. Or even inspired nonsense like "I'll forget about it, and you'll forget about it, but I'll remember, and don't you forget it . . ." Under no circumstances should you smile. Wipe that smile off your face. Who do you think you are, anyway? Who died and left you king? Who needs you? Who sent you to torment me? What have I done to deserve such a punishment? One day you will have children, and they will eat your heart out, and it will serve you right. What do we ask of you? What demands do we make? Only that you live up to your potential! That you try a little harder, that you do what you ought to do and use the brains God gave you. It isn't as if you were stupid. You're smart. Too smart for your own good. A smart mouth on you, and no sense! No judgment! What will become of you? I'll tell you what will become of you! The world will teach you a lesson! You'll get what you deserve, and if there's a heaven, I'll look down from it, and with pleasure, with heartfelt satisfaction, I'll call out to you, "You see? I told you so! All along, your parents were right." And see if you don't laugh out of the other side of your mouth then!

18. Autem, enim, igitur, demum, verum, and quoque, also vocatives, stand post-positive. A good rule, but relatively useless in adult life—how many of us have much call to translate into Latin? If, however, one uses a word like *however* or *moreover* in English, that, too, should stand post-positive. Or even *still*. Still, people break that rule all the time. And it pains you if you know the rule and see it being broken.

19. Work harder. Apply yourself and you'll be sur-

prised how easy it is. With just a little effort on your part, just a little attention, just a little change in your basic attitude, and there's no reason at all why you can't do as well as Harriet Heller. Or Warren Harshman. Or Ed Selig. (And if I became any one of those people, would you be glad? Would you love me more? Would you at least, for five minutes, stop shouting at me?)

20. Play the field. Don't tie yourself down. Don't foreclose on your opportunities. Don't saddle yourself with more than you can carry.

21. Do not remove the back of this appliance. There are high-voltage components that should only be serviced at an authorized Service Facility (see directory in the enclosed pamphlet for the facility nearest you).

22. Start off on the right foot. First impressions count. A kind word turneth away wrath. An ounce of prevention is worth a pound of cure. If you can't be good, be careful. Never apologize, never explain. Live fast, die young, and have a good-looking corpse.

23. Begin again. Turn off machine, wait thirty seconds, and restart. But can we begin again? Is there any point? Isn't there a point where the basic trust that ought to exist between two people has been killed, where there is no common ground, no place to stand, no place to hide? You think you're immune from the rules that apply to ordinary people, but you're not. And it's a lesson you ought to have learned years ago. You can't think only of yourself. You have to consider how the other person is going to feel! What were you thinking of? What did you think you were doing? Are you a person or an animal? How can you be so cavalier as to risk everything you have, to jeopardize not only your own happiness but that of your children, your entire family? How can you throw it all away like that? How did we fail you? Were you brought up to do such things? What kind of an example did we set for you? You were always so smart,

but you were never smart, had a mouth but no brain, wits but no judgment, no sense . . .

24. A pint's a pound the world around. All cats are gray in the dark. He who calls the tune must pay the piper. A stitch in time saves nine. Who lies down with dogs gets up with fleas. A dog will have his day and then, old, be unable to learn new tricks, but will bay at the moon, from a manger no doubt. Ignore this paragraph. Relax. Don't worry, be happy. If you can't be with the one you love, then love the one you're with. Don't let any of it get to you. One good way to keep from smiling and to look as though you're paying attention is to translate what they're saying into French. *Salaud! Cochon! Canaille! Morceau de merde.*

25. As long as there's life, there's hope. Words are weapons. Sticks and stones will break my bones, but words will never hurt me. (But the silver Tiffany letter opener? She can do some real damage with that!) You never know, do you? But a worm will turn. A cornered rat will fight. Hell hath no fury like a woman scorned. Jesus, this is really happening! This can't be happening. This kind of thing only happens in the movies. If you bend the wrist down, you can break almost any grip (and the letter opener does, in fact, drop, and she runs out of the room, and the wailing continues, not with words anymore, but just keening, like a siren announcing, rather belatedly, an air raid we have been enduring here for some time now.) Any port in a storm. (I call my sister, and she says to get out of there, to make tracks, to skip out the back, Jack, and make myself scarce. I take the letter opener with me, not so much as evidence but for a souvenir. And clean underwear, to avoid being run over by a bus. And dental floss and my toothbrush.) It's always darkest before the dawn. Once burned, twice careful. Practice makes perfect. A man can be judged by the company he keeps. Birds of a feather flock together. Silver should be

polished at least once a month. Always keep fifty dollars in your wallet for emergencies.

26. It's no good crying over spilt milk.

27. What's done is done.

28. A leopard can't change its spots. The day will come, young man, when you'll realize that this was good advice and that you can't ride roughshod over people's feelings. You simply cannot go on this way. If I've told you once, I've told you a thousand times! You can catch more flies with honey than you can with vinegar. (Who wants to catch flies?) If only you could learn to apply yourself, if you could pay attention, if you could learn to curb that vicious tongue of yours, if you could count to ten before you speak, if you could do unto others, if you could learn from experience . . .

29. Experience is a hard master.

30. There's no substitute for a mother's love, but young people these days seem to have no understanding, no appreciation, no sense of decency, no consideration, no remorse . . . (Oh, no, she's wrong there. Plenty of remorse!) Even so, even if you were going off to jail, even if you had killed somebody, even if your picture was on the front page of all the newspapers and you were getting what was coming to you, were getting exactly what you deserved, no less and no more, were getting your proper comeuppance, were being taught the lesson it's taken you so long to learn, you'd still be my son! Always remember that. And I'd still love you.

To My Dying Day

Isn't it your whole life that is supposed to flash before your eyes, full of half-forgotten but wonderful scenes, a rich tapestry or a busy Brueghel-like painting? He has rather been looking forward to these details, lots of them, some of them perhaps erotic. Instead, there is only this one, not-very-happy moment, just a single passage of thirty or forty seconds, as if that has been his whole life and nothing else he has achieved or experienced has even mattered.

Certainly that isn't the case. And even more disappointing is the fact that he could have remembered that moment at any time. It is not something he'd tucked away and only now recognized as important. It has always been there, saved in his consciousness, ready to flash whenever some random association triggered it. Or not so random. Every August he thinks of it on his daughter's wedding anniversary.

And now, as he lies waiting for the drug to take hold, as he lies on the bed waiting for them to come and move him to the gurney and then roll him down corridors to the operating room, there isn't any rich pageant, crowded with wonderful stuff his mind has stashed away as a treat for just this occasion. There is no sappy Frank Capra montage, but only that sordid moment at his daughter's wedding.

He's lived with that for years, knows it well, and can die with it if he has to. It is familiar at least. And if it is somewhat scruffy and disreputable, so are those teddy bears that frightened kids carry with them as they are wheeled away, along the same route to the same operating suite.

A familiar but nonetheless painful moment. He had been a guest at his daughter's wedding, and that was already painful, for he should have been the host. It should have been his name on the invitations up there with Barbara's. Even though he and Barbara were divorced, they were both still Kathie's parents. In a civilized way, they should have been able to work out some graceful and honorable arrangement for Kathie's sake and for the sake of the day.

But Barbara thought she was being handsomely accommodating by allowing him to attend at all. She thought she was doing very well simply to tolerate his presence. And she had made it clear to him that he was welcome at the wedding and at the reception afterwards. "But that is all."

"All? What do you mean? What else is there?" he asked her.

"There's nothing else. That's all."

"I don't understand what you mean. Why are you telling me this? What is it that you're spelling out for me?"

The trouble with ex-spouses is that they know each other too well, can read each other and can therefore hurt each other, knowing the other's usual defenses and weaknesses.

"The wedding is out on the lawn. The reception is also out on the lawn," Barbara explained.

"Yes? So?"

"So that's what you're invited to. Not the inside of the house."

He didn't answer her in words. He just laughed.

Which got to her, even if she tried not to let on. "You got that?" she demanded.

"Yeah, yeah," he'd said, the words afloat on a surface still rippling with his amusement.

134

Only after he'd hung up had the practical question raised itself in his mind. What if he needed to use the bathroom? What was he supposed to do, go off into the woods to pee? It was an absurd idea, but he was half tempted to call Barbara back and ask her. But only half. He resisted.

And when the day came, he carried himself well. He didn't want to embarrass Kathie. He wanted it to be a nice day for her. He couldn't blame her, after all, for her mother's eccentricities. (Well, a little, maybe. It was her wedding, and she knew how things stood between her parents and could have made some objection to Barbara's insane rules. Even now, he isn't absolutely sure she didn't try. He has never asked, because he fears the answer. Because he wants to keep at least the hope alive that Kathie wasn't a willing party to the way he was treated that day.)

It didn't help that Kathie's feminism was such that there was no part for him in the ceremony. She didn't believe in being given away, in being walked down an aisle or along a stretch of lawn and being handed over to Howie as if she were somebody's chattel.

He could see that, could understand and even agree with it, but it kept him from having any official role in the proceedings. It cut him down to the status of any observer. It cut him out.

The death of the thousand cuts: a torture, but also a reasonable description of life.

He put up with it. He kept his anger and his depression bottled up. The two evil genies. He drank very sparingly, two small glasses of champagne, one right after the ceremony and another at the toasts. The rest of the time he had club soda. Enough of which had precipitated exactly that crisis he'd expected and feared. Where to go to pee? How far into the woods?

Well, of course he wasn't going to allow the other guests to see him. He wasn't going to make a spectacle of himself just to embarrass Barbara. He was going to hide, as he'd been trained to do. As we are all trained to do. The main achievement in life is toilet training. Or, anyway, the first achievement, the thing we do to please our parents. Everything else we do is modeled somehow on that. In the laboratory as in the lavatory. The potty as trophy cup. The end of Eden, the expulsion from the garden, is the yielding of the spontaneity in our bodily functions to the demands of others.

He walked down the grassy slope to the mimosa he'd planted ten years before between the two large spruces. The gardener—no, the landscape architect!—had explained an elaborate aesthetic about not putting a showy plant in too obvious a space: "Let it hide behind something. Let it be glimpsed. Let the observer come upon it and be surprised."

Surprising, anyway, for a mimosa to survive this far north. And it had done okay up here in this cold climate, out here on the lawn. He passed it and felt a small pleasure as he might have felt had he passed an old friend. Which was what was supposed to have been happening back at the party, among all those people, so many of whom he had known back in the old days, and so few of whom had continued to talk to him after the separation and divorce. Which was another reason for being uncomfortable that day.

Okay, okay, get on with it. A little deeper into the woods. The woods are quiet, dark, and free. And I must go in there to pee. Like the flushing rules from the drought in California, from which that columnist had invented a vintage: Pouilly-pinot. (This is bad enough. What if I'd had to take a crap?) Okay, far enough in.

He looked around, looked back, and couldn't see them. So they couldn't see him. And he was about to unzip his fly. Feeling not only mortified but a failure, as if he'd peed in his pants, like Hobart Whatsis did once in the second grade. A deep sigh escaped, not quite a groan but not crying. No, really not, for the eyes were dry, swimming, brimming maybe, but not overflowing. He reached down to the zipper, and Josh said, "Dad?"

Where did he come from? Had he followed? Did he just pop up here to spy on his pop? To have to do this was bad enough, but to be seen doing it by your own son! "I have to pee," he said, as suavely and as casually as he could manage.

"Come on inside."

"I promised your mother I wouldn't."

"Never mind. Come in. I insist." Meaning that if there was any question about it later, Josh would take the responsibility—or at least try to, was willing to.

He allowed himself to be led back. In through the sun porch and the laundry room to the sand-bathroom. Josh waited in the laundry room while he peed.

And that's it. That's all. A life.

A humiliation narrowly averted. A dispensation from an unexpected quarter. A return.

Praise from his parents for going in the potty. As if they were still alive, as if they were looking down from some opening in the clouds, keeping track of their darling. To be allowed back home, even if only into a laundry room and a sand-bathroom, to be welcomed, to be loved . . .

It is the drugs. They have begun to work. They are confusing him. Those were different houses. His parents weren't his son. But they weren't all that different, were they? It was all the same, like the light that flashes over and over, the same each time, as the gurney slides along the corridor. His eyes are closed, but through the lids there are these lovely red brightenings, and he feels good, feels the relief and the gratitude as fresh as they'd been that day when his sweet son came for him deep in the woods and found him and saved him and brought him home and let him use the bathroom to pee.

137

The Impostor

I should much prefer simply to begin at some reasonable point and go forward until the end. But the facts of the case won't fit that kind of orderly presentation, no matter how much I should wish to persuade them to do so—not only for the reader's sake but to suit my own preference. I am a straightforward, down-to-earth fellow. It is my brother who is the writer. He's the one who likes to perform fancy literary tricks, with flashbacks and foreshadowings and who knows what other artful pieces of foolishness stuck here and there into what obviously would be better as a simple narrative account.

This happened and then that happened.

But, as I say, sometimes that just can't be managed. Before anything happened, there were preconditioning incidents, trivial omens. But isn't it the case that all omens look trivial? A flight of birds crosses the sky in a certain direction, and soothsayers predict the death of the emperor or even the Decline and Fall of Rome.

To be as simple and direct as I can, the first ominous puff of ill wind came some years ago, when my cousin Rochelle, leaning so far over the edge of the abyss of spinsterhood that many of us supposed her to have already fallen, found a "beau."

It was her word, and its démodé fussiness was exactly in character, too. She was not a beautiful girl (was hardly even a girl anymore in anyone's book) and was exophthalmic, so that she always looked slightly startled. Or mildly offended.

One takes one's cousins as one finds them, though. She and I had had the kind of bantering relationship that cousins often share, a tepid friendship on the surface, but underneath a messy roiling of other, rather warmer if partly repressed feelings, including envy and occasionally a touch of lust. Her bug eyes begged for that jocular goose that would give some plausible reason for her habitual expression. And like most of the women in our family, she had an admirably billowy bosom I sometimes pretended not to find fascinating.

We did nothing to violate the serious taboos and were just playing. All in good, if not quite clean, fun. Nothing actually happened between us.

Well, not quite nothing. When at last she found her Lochinvar, who had come riding out of whatever direction, we were glad for her. I include myself in that gladness. If anything, I was gladder. I had become perhaps a bit protective, which was presumptuous but nonetheless a residue of our old flirtatious closeness. I had been, as the old-fashioned phrase would have it, the friend of her youth's bosom, and my feelings for her were such that I considered myself entitled to act for her and do what a family member ought to do. Her father had died some years before Jasper's appearance. Uncle Edward's had been, in fact, the first corpse I'd ever seen, and that, too, left me with a certain odd sense of family obligation.

A suave and genial fellow, Jasper seemed to know everything and to have been everywhere. It was not merely my rudimentary jealousy, which conceivably may have played some small part, but my pride that was offended. He dropped names, places, and even labels, not merely to display his own breadth of experience and superiority of taste and judgment, but defiantly, aggressively, letting you know that he was testing yours. Whatever it was, he knew about it, had been there, was a friend of the chef, grew up with the comptroller of the company, and so on.

In short, he was annoying. And he was bolder in some of his claims than any sensible impostor would have been. Had he, for instance, contented himself with a Bronze Star, a Silver Star, or even a Distinguished Flying Cross, I'd have believed him. I might not have liked it, but I should have assumed that there had been some brief moment of authenticity before the later posturing and preening.

But the Congressional Medal of Honor? That was too much, and too easy to check—which, of course, I did, calling first the local public library and then the Pentagon. Nobody had any record of his ever having been given that rare decoration. He claimed to have won it for the development of skip bombing in the Pacific in World War II.

I can't remember now who developed skip bombing, but it wasn't Jasper.

This was disturbing because it called into question his other, more modest claims, which none of us had ever thought to challenge. He had not attended the University of Missouri, I discovered, either as an undergraduate or as a student in their school of journalism. There was no record of his ever having been enrolled. Neither was he listed in the Social Register. (What a silly thing to boast about when it could be so easily disproved!) No father, or at least none of the same last name, had owned horses that raced at Saratoga in the years before World War II.

He was a fake. But when the family confronted Rochelle not only with these distressing bits of information but with the further revelation from an uncle of ours that Jasper had been married at least twice before and had served three years in a state prison for embezzlement, all she had to say was that the love of a good woman would surely redeem him.

Bosomy enough, she had never been what one would call an intellectual. Still, I was appalled by this manifestation of a vulgarity I had tried for so long to overlook. It was also irksome that she was not grateful to us for our exertions in her behalf. She was angry at me for having begun this tawdry business, which had led to Uncle Charlie's hiring of that private detective and Jasper's exposure as a twice divorced ex-con. I was not apologetic. I insisted that I had been doing her a kindness.

High on my horse, I even declared that I would never have anything to do with Jasper and that I would not attend their wedding if she was so foolish as to go ahead and marry this bounder. Indeed, if she was going to be that stupid, neither my brother nor I would have anything more to do with her, I said, although I had no warrant to speak for my brother, who was at the American Academy in Rome that year, having won some literary fellowship. I wrote to him, but he had no idea why I'd allowed myself to get involved or why I was so exercised about what was essentially none of my business.

Rochelle ignored my ridiculous threats and married Jasper, and he may or may not have been redeemed by the love of a good woman. Quite conceivably, a mere reluctance to return to prison was what had so settling and salutary an effect. At any rate, he went straight, or relatively so, taking a job in advertising—where his braggart's knack was an asset. He and Rochelle have lived together in comparative peace and affection for some years now, although I do not see them, nor they me, except at funerals.

A flight of birds in a certain direction across the sky. Is it only an isolated and absurd and altogether irrelevant happening?

I am no mystic. That, too, is rather more in my brother's line. But I do remember thinking about Jasper and Rochelle—about Jasper, anyway—a few years later when, in Miami, I was a guest at a large garden party. It had promised to be a tedious gathering, a business meeting imperfectly disguised as a social occasion, and I was there to represent the company I work for. We had come down for a long weekend for an industrial show in Miami, which in February is a pleasant change from the rigors of Pennsylvania. That a few of us had been assigned to attend this boring party was scarcely a hardship. The estate (one can call it nothing less) belonged to the chairman of the board of a firm that supplied our company with certain electronic components, and as Fred Clavering and I presented ourselves at the gate, I remember my reaction to the lavish landscaping, a peculiar combination of jungle luxuriance and artifactual fussiness. It all seemed unreal, a strenuous joke, although without discernible point. The effect was somehow unsettling, making one feel just a little giddy. Or silly. We were greeted by a crew of junior executives of our host's company, stationed at a table beneath a candy-striped awning at the foot of a drive so long that we could not glimpse any part of the main house from where we stood. A young woman asked our names, and we answered—correctly, of course.

She consulted her list and found us, but her hand must have strayed as she reached among the rows of lapel badges set out on the table before her, for she drew the wrong name tag and fastened it to my jacket lapel.

Had I noticed the mistake, I surely would have corrected it at once.

Of course I would have corrected it. I am not the kind of fellow who goes around impersonating Italian nobility.

But I was unaware of what had happened until some minutes later when we were already mingling with the guests, who milled decorously about the manicured lawn under huge banyan trees with the blue glitter of Biscayne Bay behind us.

I had been well treated, of course. At such a function, one expects to be treated well. Even with a certain deference.

But I was like a pretty girl at a prom. People were positively flocking about me, especially women, and that was unusual. At length one woman addressed me as Count Whoever, and I smiled and pointed to my lapel badge, intending to correct her gently with my right name.

I looked down and saw that the badge proclaimed me to be Il Conto Giacomo de Verdura.

Not wanting to embarrass her, I didn't laugh.

The Count of Vegetables?

(On the other hand, as I later discovered, there is such a title. It is Sicilian. Italians have a peculiar sense of what is grand.)

Not having my real name to offer, I told the young woman I never use my title and was surprised when the people who made up these badges had slapped it on me like an ad on a billboard.

It was as if I had opened my wallet and displayed a patent of nobility. She believed it absolutely.

She believed me.

And as I was standing there, harmlessly impersonating some scion of the brilliant and venerable Vegetable family, I thought of Jasper.

I realized there was a kind of fun, a peculiar liveliness and intensity, that comes with imposture. It wasn't, as I would otherwise have supposed, the mean triumph of one person's will over another's gullibility. It was gentler than that. There was a collaborative and communal satisfaction that, together, my audience and I were creating a wholly new existence out of nothing more than a flack's mistake.

It was, I came to realize, an art form, an imposition

not just on a few strangers at a garden party but on the world itself, on the limitations of a material existence where one is cast in a role one must play forever, no doubt to the eternal boredom even of the Creator.

In a series of intoxicating improvisations, I found myself inventing answers to ordinary social inquiries and amazing myself. I said I was a member of the faculty of the University of Bologna, that I was here on a Barberini fellowship to study American management practices, and that I had viticultural holdings in Tuscany.

At one point someone challenged me and suggested that my accent wasn't typically Italian. I explained that I had learned English in the Berlitz School in Turin and that my instructor had been a native of Athol, Mass., which is, in fact, a city I have never visited. The name just popped into my head. My only association with it was from the punchline of an old and rather cruel campaign joke about Endicott Peabody being the first man to run for the office of governor of Massachusetts who had four towns of that commonwealth named after him: Endicott, Peabody, Marblehead, and Athol. The mind is wonderfully productive. I had apparently filed that tidbit away under the general category of nonsense, which certainly covered my activities as an impostor of the Italian nobility.

I was rather good at it, I think. It certainly felt good. It was exhilarating, as if I were drawing on a canvas and each new stroke added another dimension to the already interesting figure that emerged on the easel before me. But it was better than that, for these other people, the party, the absurd landscaping itself, provided the medium on which I made these deft and telling daubs.

Fred, whose name tag accurately proclaimed his identity, was horrified, and he wandered away, distancing himself from what he considered to be aberrant behavior. I suppose it was. Most people give their real names, answer truthfully the questions of strangers, and are straightforward and reliable as they expect others to be.

But that is what makes it fun to depart on occasion from the tedious details of one's actual dossier, trying new data as one tries on clothing in a store, experimenting with a new appearance, a whole new persona. What harm was there? Whom was I injuring or defrauding? At the worst, there were a few people who remembered an odd count from Italy who jabbered too energetically. Anyone my performance bored was free to go for a refill from the punch bowl or the coffee urn and not return.

Fred was alarmed, concerned about what he took to be a manifestation of a dangerous tendency that must have lain buried somewhere within me all along, a treacherous flaw he was only now discovering that ran only God knew how deep. I was a colleague with whom he had worked for years, a man he thought he could trust. Now I was threatening him, calling into question the stability of the world on which he depended, in which he made his living. This was clearly at risk if the man in the next office could transform himself at any instant into an altogether different person. Had I kept hidden away in the trunk of my car all these years a tam o'shanter and a kilt? A cowboy suit? A menacing leather jacket of the kind that members of motorcycle gangs affect?

And in a way, he was right to feel alarmed. Because everything we do in the world of business depends on contracts and their implicit promises. Not only will you perform in thus and such a way with thus and such materials, but you will continue from day to day to be the same person, answering to the same name, being responsible and dependable. Which is what makes the alternative so appealing. To start fresh, to chuck all this, even if only for a little while, and try a new tack on a new sea and in a new vessel!

Fred was so upset that he did not even question or criticize me. There was no trace of that high-minded expression of disapproval I had expected. My behavior had been so grotesque as to be beyond censure—or else there was something within him that responded, that was fascinated by what I'd done. That, too, was possible.

The worst I had to fear was that he'd tell other people in the firm or that he might make some official report. But the schoolboy code was too much ingrained in him, and he didn't peach on me.

I suppose I should have worried more about the risks I had run, but I was more occupied by my delight in what I'd managed to do. An amazing thing to consider, that ability to change, to improvise, to create on the spur of the moment something new, something never even thought of before! It was also amazing to discover that I had a talent, not like my brother's but quite different, and in some ways even more interesting.

"What's past is prologue," Shakespeare says. (But if I had written, " 'What's past is prologue,' Milton tells us," would you have known?)

The reason for the scrupulousness that certain people display about accuracy and truthfulness is their understanding that by a stroke of the pen they can undo the world, and they are reluctant or perhaps afraid of the chaos that will follow. I was fascinated by the chaos. I found, however, that my realization of my power—the power we all have if only we are bold enough to think of exercising it—did not admit of trifles. I understood that I had a genie in a bottle, but I was not going to call upon it for ridiculous favors, for out-of-season raspberries or similar poignant bits of domestic legerdemain.

The fairy tales are correct, however, in the way they show the hero wasting his first couple of wishes. The simple youth must be made to understand the power he commands.

But having been the Count de Verdura, if for only an hour or so, I already comprehended that power. I knew what serious issues were involved in this *jeu d'esprit*—issues, indeed, of the spirit. I had tried the divine gift of metamorphosis, had stolen something better than the gods' thunder. I had performed Proteus' trick. Or Zeus's, for that matter.

Is this how my brother would describe it? Am I becoming too literary?

I don't know. I never discussed these matters with him. They were too important to dissipate in chat, which is what writers never understand. I didn't want merely to be amusing. That, too, was a kind of trivialization I wished to avoid. Life is not raw material for something else—literature or art—but primary, the real thing. In our little circuses, the artists are the clowns at the fringes of the main arena, diverting us while the trapeze artists and animal trainers prepare to risk everything.

Look here, you say. Get to the point. What happened next?

Nothing happened.

Which is why I'm vamping this way, allowing some time to pass. Or at least suggesting that my waiting had an effervescent quality to it. I didn't impersonate anyone, nor did I start sending pseudonymous letters or making crank phone calls. I invented no new existences for myself. Such things would have been contrived and, if I may venture a literary judgment, trite.

But eventually something must have happened! After the time passed, then what?

Well, as time passed, I digested these earlier events, preparing myself for the moment when the right opportunity should at last arrive—as, of course, it did. In some mountain fastness in West Virginia, a place I had never seen or even heard of, there was a flash flood. It was more remote than Athol. The flood there was one of those things we note on television newscasts with only perfunctory interest. Sad, yes, but what has it to do with us, with our lives?

What, indeed? It was a bad storm. Not only were the roads impassable, but the telephone lines were out, too. And although I'd had no idea that this was so, my brother was there in that very town. He and another writer were doing a series of readings together in West Virginia, Maryland, and Pennsylvania and were now stranded at some cow college, entirely cut off from the rest of the world.

I hadn't worried about him because I'd had no idea he was there until the call came through to tell me he was all right but that his travel plans were shot to hell.

So? What was important about the disturbance of my brother's travel plans? What had this to do with me?

The odd wrinkle in the usually smooth surface of things was that my brother's wife had been out running some errand or other. Without telephone service, the only communication from this West Virginian hamlet had been by ham radio, and because I am reliably at my office and available, my brother's second attempt at a patched phone call had been to me, to let me know what was happening and then to ask me to relay the news to my sister-in-law, Bridget. He also asked me to telephone another college near Gettysburg, Pennsylvania, where he and his companion, a not very well known poet I shall call Bell, were due to appear the following day. I was to explain to them why the reading had to be canceled and to convey regrets.

I agreed, of course, and the improvised connection—none too good at any time—either failed or was deliberately ended. I replaced the phone on its cradle as carefully as if it were a live thing, for I recognized the arrival of that moment toward which all these earlier events had been quietly tending. I was not commanded. I could decline, if I chose. But I was invited. I could, if I cared to or dared to, step through Alice's looking glass and experience a divine thrill of creation that my brother, the scribbler, had never imagined.

I made hurried excuses at the office, telling them that a family emergency had arisen, I'd be gone for the rest of the day, and I might or might not be able to come in on the morrow. But I would surely be in the day after that. I went home and packed. I called Bridget to let her know her husband was all right.

She had not been worried. But I'd done my duty.

I called several bookstores before I located a volume of Bell's poems. It seemed to me wrong to try to impersonate my own brother, too easy and perhaps incestuous. But this other fellow, a man I'd never met, never even heard of . . .

I found his slender collection, inspected it, and found it to be plausible enough. A publication of a university press, it was a severe little production with praise on the back from luminaries I'd never heard of. No photograph, of course—that cost money. I examined the contents to determine whether they, too, were suitable, for I had certain requirements about the poems I'd be reading. They could be neither terrible nor amazingly good and therefore intimidating. I needed a text that avoided both extremes.

It was fascinating how clear I was about certain of these details. I discovered I had an instinct for them, an innate aptitude. It was uncanny, as if I had learned in some other life what was necessary to do or important to avoid. I paid and left the shop. I felt as efficient and inexorable as a sci-fi robot.

There were some surprises, however. I was unprepared for the delay, for the arduousness of getting through the hours of anticipation. The inevitable calculation was quite different from my breezily impromptu experience in Miami. I kept asking myself what I had neglected to plan for. What steps could I take to protect myself? More important, this novel period of preparation carried with it a new kind of moral challenge or burden. I was now committed to something not unlike an assignation, which is altogether a different thing from a serendipitous erotic encounter. Or, to change metaphors and exaggerate only a little, it was like the difference between manslaughter, in the heat of the moment, and premeditated murder, which involves what the legal profession calls "malice prepense."

I was experiencing something akin to what performing artists must feel as they sit in their dressing rooms waiting for their calls. Writers, too, as they confront, first thing in the morning, the stupid blankness of an empty page daring them to try once more the old business of incantation. Can their muttered syllables summon a spirit and then, wonder upon wonder, corporealize it from wraith into living creature, indistinguishable from the spectators around the campfire or in the tavern or at the fairground?

That snowdrift glare of the page is intimidating enough, but how much worse, how much more frightening, is the prospect of working the magic on living creatures? The magician, to show how good he really is, leaves off toying with coins, ropes, colored handkerchiefs, and metal hoops and at a certain point in the performance graduates to rabbits, pigeons, poodles, and even tigers and elephants in a grand finale that astonishes us all. But I would be working even higher on the evolutionary ladder, with human beings no less! I had nothing up my sleeve, nothing under my hat but my head and its fancies, and from these I would attempt to create not only a credible person but a passable artist, a figure as worthy of the attention of these students as the real Bell could be.

Throwing my Gladstone bag into the back seat, I set out and headed, Greeley-wise, to the west. With the pleasant monotony of the turnpike to induce a trancelike state, I was able to consider once more the project on which I had embarked. Most artists claim to have a certain vocation, to have been visited by a muse, to be distinguished from their ordinary fellows by some special grace or curse. What I was doing was on my own hook, through my own volition. It was yet another imposition of my will on the world.

Or was it? Could one not as easily suppose that the miscalculation of Jasper's silly boast and then the minimal error of the public relations woman at that estate in Miami when I got Il Conto's name tag were gears in an intricate machine by which the fates were working their will upon me?

Ridiculous! A little boy's absurd speculation. It was a part, though, of a wonderful boyishness, the energy and keen liveliness I felt, an elixir of youth and vigor of amazing efficacy. The drive was a delight with fancies gathering about me like clouds before a summer storm. I was one little speck in the stream of traffic, but a maverick, for all the rest of them were presumably engaged in prosaic enterprises, meeting with clients or lugging sample cases from one buyer to the next. Or so it seemed in the daylight. The approach of darkness, however, suggested other, richer possibilities. As the headlights of the cars switched on, their occupants were somehow enlivened. Might not at least some of them be meeting illicit lovers? Were the slower drivers carefully obeying the posted speed limit in order not to be stopped by the police cruisers because they did not want the drugs in their trunks to be discovered? Why not allow them as much freedom as I was now claiming for myself and suppose that a certain number of them were on their way to make fraudulent appearances in one unpredictable capacity or another, just for the sport of it? Suppose that only one car in a hundred was being driven by an impostor of some kind, and in the stream of cars across the median strip there was, cumulatively, an impressively large contingent of us! And nobody else knew, even suspected, because mostly we do it successfully.

These were hardly my usual thoughts. But that, too, was an interesting phenomenon. In my decision to become Mr. Bell, I had to some degree abandoned my usual self and had become someone new—not Bell, by any means, but a creature altogether without precedent, what biologists and perhaps philosophers, too, would call a sport. Which was reassuring. The newer, the better. Or was there a part of me that wanted to get away from this unseemly and embarrassing foolishness? If I was not my old fuddy-duddy self, then it was not so intimately involved.

The devil made me do it! An irresistible impulse! A divine inspiration! There is a truth in those claims, an admission that men and women are not always rational beings but are subject to influences and promptings they do not necessarily understand and sometimes cannot resist. We fear these moments, but they also enlarge us, making us vessels of something grand and glorious—or terrible.

Hours had passed, and I had to stop to get gasoline. But I was neither tired nor hungry. I thought a drink might do me good in a medicinal way, letting me slow down the racing of my thoughts so that I could be fresh in the morning when I showed up as Bell at the little college and made excuses for my missing partner.

(Excuses? What excuses? Instantly I invented for my brother a slight concussion from which he seemed to have recovered. But the doctors wanted to keep him under observation for another day or so. His car, though, was a total loss. Still, we were lucky. All this came unbidden and fully formed, popping out of my forehead as amazingly as Athena sprang from the brow of Zeus.)

At length I reached the right exit and found a cluster of motels of soothing anonymity. Their recognizable names and logos plucked the intersection from its setting and set it down as an interchangeable unit that might have been anywhere and was therefore nowhere. After a couple of drinks, a dinner, and a hot bath, I was ready for the dreamland alternative to my real life, one dream yielding to another for the moment. It was hardly worth giving so much time to unconsciousness. But perhaps I might dream of my wife, my job, my children, the ordinary and the exotic having for the moment changed places.

Everything was funny, rich, charged. The watercolors of Montmartre with which the room had been embellished seemed to me almost hysterically amusing. The wooden object against the wall, part dresser, part desk, part television stand, was so utilitarian as to be heartbreaking and precious. The hum of a fan blended antiphonally with the distant continuo of the turnpike traffic, as if motion and stasis were singing together, yearning for each other. Everything had a voice, a message, a meaning—as, of course, it probably does to real poets who are possessed this way from time to time. (Not always, I hope, for that would surely drive them mad, but now and again so that they learn not to trust too much to the surfaces of things. Which, of course, they also celebrate, valuing them precisely because they cannot take them for granted. The colors and textures and smells that are so treacherous, that are like the bodies and faces of fascinating women whom it would be folly to trust but impossible not to love.)

And then, in the wink of a hat, I was sleeping a blessedly dreamless sleep.

In the morning, I awoke knowing just what to do. After I had breakfasted and checked out, I drove to the college, passed its gate without even slowing down, and continued for a quarter of a mile or so until I found a place where I could leave the car. I grabbed my bag and walked back to present myself to the college.

Doctor Walker, the rather wide, somewhat squat chairwoman of the English department, was in her middle fifties but still a woman of some style, in a tailored suit with a black silk blouse and a gaudy scarf tied about her neck in studied carelessness. Having been ushered into her office as soon as I gave Bell's name, I shook her proffered hand and seated myself in the indicated chair.

I recited the story I had prepared—about how our car had been involved in an accident, my traveling companion had suffered minor injuries and was being held for observation in a county hospital some hundred miles distant, and I had hitchhiked most of the night to arrive here to fulfill our obligation.

She was, of course, eager to do whatever she could to be helpful to me and to the writer with whom I had been touring. I assured her that my fellow artist was in good hands. His brother from Philadelphia—that is, myself—had been summoned and was on his way. (I knew the delight Hitchcock must have experienced walking a poodle across the frame in a street scene of one of his films, an apparently innocuous figure, almost comic, but nevertheless the culprit, the man who in the truest sense of the words "did it.")

For myself, I told her I should be grateful for a place where I could take a nap for a few hours. And if it could be located, a copy of any of my earlier books. Stupidly, I'd left my briefcase behind in the trunk of the damaged vehicle, and all my books were in it except one copy of the new one that I'd packed separately. And alas, my portfolio of new poetry was also missing. No, it was not an utter catastrophe—there were copies of these poems at home—but I was afraid I should have to limit myself in the reading to published material.

Dr. Walker made a couple of telephone calls while her secretary produced coffee for me. Eventually one Linda McKenzie came in, an assistant professor who would have been pretty if she had given herself half a chance. She wore a denim skirt and a black leather jacket and mirror sunglasses as if she were a member of a street gang rather than a college faculty. I wondered whether it was an honor for her or a menial duty that she had been deputized to look after visiting writers. At any rate, she had an apartment on campus and could offer me her daybed. Would I be up to meeting a class that afternoon, though, Dr. Walker wanted to know.

I assured them that after only a brief nap I should be quite pleased to meet with a class of young writers, that it would, in fact, be soothing after the shock of the previous night's events.

They asked for the details, and I embellished my story a little, telling them how we had swerved to avoid a deer and the car had gone into a skid and hit a tree. We had not been traveling at a very great speed and had hit glancingly and bounced off. Still, the impact had caused my friend to hit his head on the door on his left. It could have been much worse. We had been lucky.

"You must be exhausted," Dr. Walker said. "I mustn't keep you any longer."

I was dismissed. But I had succeeded, at least so far. The hardest part was behind me. No one had stared at me and laughed; no one had announced, "You are an impostor." It was not probable, but it had always been a possibility that one of them might know Bell by sight. It was still conceivable that somebody could challenge me. Indeed, that was what made this exciting, made the blood course and the mind race just a little faster. I was actually feeling the fatigue I had attributed to myself, as if I had really been up all night and out on the road.

Professor McKenzie—Linda, she insisted—led me along a corridor and out a rear door to the parking lot where her pickup truck was parked. Outdoorswoman? Radical lesbian? Or was she merely making a sixtyish statement that was vaguely egalitarian or populist? Her apartment smelled of cats and was also making a statement. She was a writer of short stories, had published a couple of collections of these things, and was now working on a novel. She announced this to me, it seemed, as much to foreclose as to invite conversation. I nodded and told her I was exhausted. The daybed was possible, but there was cat hair on it. I could sleep in her bed, she offered. If I kept the door closed, the cats wouldn't bother me. I told her I'd prefer that if she didn't mind.

"Why should I mind?" she asked.

Perhaps she was just unmindful not only of the way she dressed or the way her apartment, none too tidy to begin with, smelled of the cats and their litter box, but of the whole physical world. Most people of whichever sex consider it a form of intimacy to invite another person into their bed, even if only to sleep. It seemed to me curious to be offered her unmade bed, empty, of course, but with her wraith still there in the wrinkles of her impress. I hung my jacket on the back of her chair and started to unbutton my shirt, wondering at what point she'd back away and close the door. I had the shirt off and had begun to undo my belt before she said she'd wake me in a couple of hours and she closed the door behind her.

Not bad looking. Lean and leggy, but so absurdly vague! Her mind presumably was full of complicated thoughts about literature—or perhaps that was what her colleagues supposed. My own guess was that she was just a little loose in the wiring somewhere. I laid my pants on her desk and crawled into her bed to lie there—quite agreeably surprised, for I was no longer a figure in my own fantasy but a toy of the fates. I had made my lie and I was bedded in it—or was that one of those intricate pieces of foolishness my brother might try to get away with and that I usually have no patience for? Was I going a bit soft in the head? Or was it just the giddiness of the successful imposture and the anticipation of the next unpredictable scene?

Would she, for example, forget I was there in her room and her bed and come in for a nap? No, of course not. I realized I had to be careful and keep a tight rein on myself. It would be ruinous to be lulled by the first easy steps of this adventure. I still had to face a series of scrutinizing audiences, picadors to the bull I was about to throw them. At any moment, some smart kid or resentful faculty member might pull the rug out from under me, asking me an elementary technical question the answer to which I didn't know, and then, in the gales of derisive laughter that would follow, I'd be unmasked . . .

Amazingly, I fell asleep. In Linda's bed, as if I had actually been up most of the night hitchhiking to the college and was exhausted from my exertions, I drifted off into a dreamless sleep. It was when I awoke that I returned to dreamland, for I felt hands on my shoulders that were jostling me and I looked up, not into my wife's face but into that of a stranger. Linda? Yes, of course, Linda McKenzie. It came rushing back, as headlong as one of those famous Bay of Fundy tides.

"Want some coffee?" she asked. "You've got to do a class in forty minutes."

"Oh, yes. Please. Black with a little sugar."

"You mind instant?"

I ordinarily do, but the poet might not. The good guest certainly wouldn't. "No, no, that'll be fine."

I waited until she went off to the kitchen, then got out of her bed and put on my trousers. She brought the coffee in an oversized cup, one of those gaily glazed pieces of folk pottery from Portugal or Italy.

"You're very kind," I said.

She shrugged off the compliment. Or maybe it was a shrug of incomprehension, as though there weren't any conceivable alternatives.

"You're older than I thought you'd be," she said.

SHORT STORIES ARE NOT REAL LIFE

Naturally I was worried. "I began publishing late," I said. "Like Frost. You're not disappointed, I hope."

She shook her head. "I'm not, no. We usually get these young people coming through with their first books tucked under their arms. Because the department can't pay much, I guess. I'm happy to see somebody older. A grown-up, I mean. I like it that you're the age you are."

"Good," I said, taking another sip.

"You want a little brandy in that?" she offered.

"Why not?"

It was California brandy, a little raw maybe but okay in the instant coffee. She poured some for herself into a Muppets glass and drank it without coffee. "Ready?" she asked.

And off I went as Mr. Bell—a ringer, anyway—to tell the kiddies about life and art, to play coy as I have often enough heard my brother do, refusing to explicate his poems, allowing any interpretation by any reader to stand on an equal footing with his own. Or pretending to. It forestalls attacks from unreconstructed deconstructionists and also seems modest, although it's obviously a false modesty. If anyone in these English departments really believed that deconstructionist stuff, they wouldn't be inviting writers to come and address their classes. Critics would have it all to themselves.

But okay. I don't mind a little craziness and bad faith. It only makes life easier for the itinerant fraud like myself. I took positions I thought were least liable to pass unchallenged but weren't altogether boring. I allowed schools a place in the training of young writers, but I said there were other and maybe more important things to do, like having a pet or a garden. And if one were to study in classrooms, it shouldn't be literature but one of those other subjects that refined one's powers of observation: history of art or of music, or any of the biological sciences.

"You don't think writing courses are important?" one

young woman asked. She was glowering, unsure whether to be belligerent or not. She had one of those highlighters so that lines in her notebook as well as passages in her textbooks were striped yellow, as if she were contagious and had infected printed words with a weird tropical disease.

"Byron never took writing courses," I told her. "Or Pope. Or Milton. Or Dickens."

"Isn't that a facile answer?" she wanted to know.

"I don't know," I said, "but it's true, isn't it?"

It wasn't a particularly dramatic exchange, but it was about as heated as any I can remember, and it was the only time I had the least uneasiness about anyone leaping to her feet to expose me as an impostor and mountebank. No such thing happened. The class was so responsible and reasonable as to approach dullness, although some of the discredit properly belongs to me. The students sat there too eager to write down in their notebooks the platitudes I had to offer them—simplified versions, or not so simplified maybe, of things I'd heard my brother say when he was in the mood to pontificate. But they were just kids. I was talking to myself as much as to them when I complained about how few readers there were, how lonely the life of the artist was in contemporary America, how uncertain the financial rewards—all the usual gripes. As a valediction, I advised them to sponge off their parents for as long as possible and then to marry money, and that was another emotional high point because they assumed I was being antifeminist and condescending. I wasn't. My brother had married Bridget because he loved her, but he had allowed himself to fall in love with her because she had money. This isn't sexist at all, but only intelligent.

After class, there was a cocktail party and then a small dinner at a table for twelve that had been set up in a faculty dining room off the larger student refectory. And then, at last, there was the reading in a large auditorium that was hardly half full. It wasn't me, I had to remind myself; it wasn't my reading that they were so indifferent to, but I was a bit put out nonetheless. It was a part of my generalized notion of the imposture—or the performance, which was how I thought of it—that there should be a sizable audience, a sea of people out there, and this group of perhaps two dozen was a barely minimal fulfillment of what the scenario called for.

Or to put it another way, to achieve the giddiness I wanted, I had to take greater risks. If I was not going to perform before hundreds, then what I did with my tens would have to be all the more daring and defiant. I could have been satisfied with a simple swan dive if it had been from the top of that cliff in Acapulco, but from an ordinary high board into a pool, there had to be twists and somersaults to achieve that same ambitious score. It was not sufficient just to stand there, read Bell's poems, nod my head in gratitude for the polite applause, and get off the stage. No, I had to be an artist, a performing personality they would remember, whose charm would be such that they would prefer the persona to the actual literary artifacts I had brought them.

Because of my brother, I'd been to a few poetry readings, enough anyway to know that one cannot simply read a barrage of little lyrics. There has to be a breathing space between the poems, a chance for the audience to recover and to regroup for the demands that the next poem is going to make on their attention. It is necessary to talk, even if only meaningless blather, to keep the poems from running together into an aural blur. And that was my opportunity, where I could allow myself the room to beguile a little. And take risks.

I began actually to talk about imposture, to admit that the reading poet was not at all the same as the composing poet, that there were at least three: the original creator, the improving editor, and—least interesting—the performer, who was only distantly related to the poet in whom the audience ought to be interested.

"As if the man before you were not the Bell you had invited but, say, his brother, who knows him, of course, but who is not altogether reliable. No poet is a reliable witness to the conception of his own poem. If the poem is any good, he's too busy conceiving it to notice much of what's going on. It's not a moment of acute self-awareness. And if the poem is not any good, then his testimony is not of very great interest, is it? I have no recollection at all, for example, of the circumstances of the composition of this next poem," I said, quite accurately, and proceeded to the next poem in Bell's book.

And once more, just before the last poem, I touched upon the true theme of my appearance, suggesting to my listeners that the speaking voice in each poem was not necessarily my own and that they ought to listen as if I were doing a series of dramatic readings, as if there were no man named Bell but a passer-by who had dropped in to entertain them. "Actually, you don't know who I am, anyway," I said. "I might be an impostor, which would be an interesting fiction, whether it was true or not. The only truth as far as we are concerned here is the truth of art, after all, which is on an altogether different plane."

Was there a raised eyebrow? I'm afraid not. I think they rather expected their poets to say quirky things, to be a bit silly. They dislike poets, I suspect. Poets are like spinach farmers, who produce stuff they have to ingest because it's supposed to be good for them. And some of them might even have liked it if they'd ever given it a chance—or been given a chance themselves. But poems, for them, are hoops to jump through, treacherous occasions for an intellectual performance upon which they are going to be graded. My brother grouses about it often enough.

I read the last poem, the last one in Bell's book. If he

figured it was good to end with, then I'd trust him. Poets ought to be at least as smart as grocers and put the good pieces at the front and at the back where they'll attract prospective buyers. This poem was about going back to the town he'd lived in as a child and resenting whatever had changed, as if the whole place ought to have been turned into a kind of shrine to his having lived there, but what was interesting was how Bell had set it up so that his own memories and perceptions were turned against him.

It was, at any rate, satisfactory. I was able to read it with conviction and enough of a finishing flourish to win a polite hand. And then there was coffee and cider and cookies and an opportunity for me to talk with the students, very few of whom had any interesting questions. When had I published my first poems? How many poems did one have to have to make a book manuscript? Did one need an agent for poetry? Could one make a living as a poet? (To the last question I answered no, and said I was an engineer and designed electronic sensors and quality control devices— which is close to the truth.)

The issue of imposture that had been raised in my performance did not seem to have interested any of them. No one asked why I'd been talking about it, what I was getting at, or why I'd been harping on that string. It didn't come up at all until afterward, when the party began to break up and I asked Linda if she could give me a lift.

"But where?" she asked. "The last bus has already left. There's nothing out of here until tomorrow morning."

I hesitated. Where was I going to spend the night? In a guest apartment the college could provide? Back in Linda McKenzie's apartment and bedroom? Was that her invitation? If it was, could I consider exploiting this impersonation and accepting?

"I left my car a mile or so down the road," I said.

"But I thought—"

"Yes, I know," I said. "It was a fiction. I'll explain on the way."

She shrugged. I said goodbye to Dr. Walker and to the small group of students who remained and followed Linda McKenzie to her pickup truck.

"Which way?" she asked, and I pointed.

"Not very far," I told her, encouragingly.

"I don't understand."

"The simple explanation," I said, "is that I'm not Bell. I'm a faker. An impostor. I heard that they'd been cut off in a flood, and I thought it would be fun to try something like this. It's something I've wanted to do for years, but have never had a chance. And here it was, handed to me, a perfect opportunity."

Nothing. No reaction at all.

"You're angry?" I asked. "You have a right to be."

"I don't believe you," she said.

"Okay. I won't argue. I prefer it that way."

"I think you're a nut, but I think you're Bell."

"Okay," I said. "There, that's my car."

She slowed, stopped, and reached into her purse.

"And here's your check," she said. "Or Bell's check."

"I'll see that he gets it," I promised.

She shook her head and shrugged. "A nice reading, though, whoever you are."

"Thanks." I waved. She put the truck into gear, executed a neat U-turn, and sped away.

In those odd, ghostly hours after midnight, as I negotiated my way back through the empty, moonlit miles to Philadelphia, I realized that I had perhaps achieved something satisfying: there was at least a theoretical possibility that Linda McKenzie or Dr. Walker or one of the other members of that audience might one day see a picture of Jason Bell, remember what I looked like, and figure out that, hey, wait, that was a different guy. I had set a time bomb, a kind of booby trap that might go off at any time if only the right conditions were met.

And poems and novels and short stories are just like that, devices that may explode at some future time, that are designed to discharge their burden of meaning and emotion whenever the right reader comes along to trip the wires in his head.

This observation was interesting in itself, but it was also an intermediate step toward a further understanding of my all but involuntary behavior of the previous couple of days—that perhaps I had done it right, had, in fact, succeeded beyond my wildest dreams, having created in my own way a work of art.

In that regard I was better off than most poets and also better off than most frauds and fakers, for they have to keep on doing it, are obliged to repeat that exhilarating experience. The biographies of impersonators are not usually written and studied, but the lives of poets and novelists and short story writers are well enough known, and no one ever thinks to ask why it is that they do their trick again and again, as if there were no satisfaction in having already done it well, or as if the benefit of their performance ended almost as soon as they had put their pencils down.

Linda hadn't believed my confession. She supposed something much worse—that I was rejecting her diffident invitation or was wriggling free even before she'd actually managed to extend it. My sister-in-law didn't believe my account of my adventure either, but that's another story.

My brother loved it, but was a little put out that I'd decided to be Bell. If I was going to impersonate a poet, why couldn't I have kept it in the family and impersonated him?

"For the otherness," I explained. "Is everything you write literally true? Doesn't it give you a kick to invent new stuff, to get far away from your own experience? Don't you ever invent when you write?"

"Sure, but—"

"Me, too. You would have been too close, and that would have diminished the trick of it!"

He scratched his head. He could see what I was getting at, but he still couldn't imagine me actually buying the book and getting in the car, going off to do it. No, no, it was not in my character. It was fine that I had thought up such a preposterous tale. But I could not expect him to believe I'd carried it out.

So it bothered the hell out of him when I gave him the check made out to Jason Bell from that little college he and Bell were supposed to have read at. "Send it on to Bell," I told him. "Let him cash it or not, as he sees fit."

He stared at it, stared at me, looked back at the check, and then started to laugh. "Maestro!" he said.

And he hugged me. Like a brother.

Something She Touched

Other families do these things better. Or maybe they mess up, too, but in ways that only they can understand. Maybe from their vantage point we would look as if we knew what we were doing.

But we don't know. We grope clumsily. At funerals, for instance, there are passionate arguments, and the passion never has anything to do with the subject of the dispute. Does it matter a whole lot whether the people who shovel the earth into the grave have the blade of the shovel turned upside down or not? Does rabbinical lore address this question? Is it ritual, or was it merely the custom in whatever eastern European village we fled from?

Lois takes these things very seriously. She likes nothing better than to correct rabbis, demonstrating not only her learning but also her connection with God, which she thinks is closer than anyone else's. It's infuriating—the predictable result, I suppose, of an unhappy adolescence. She was happy enough as a child, but puberty was unkind to her. She got fat and blimpy, and as a high-school girl she must have suffered. She looked, as even her mother told her, like a horse. It wasn't so much her being overweight as it was a certain clumsiness, a heavy gait and a dopey expression I can still remember, even though that's all gone now. She has lost weight and looks better, now that she's married and has two children, than she could ever have expected. But the heaven to which she turned in her lonely teenage desperation remains an important part of her life. She married Morris, an orthodox crazy. They have timing devices on their refrigerator so that their opening of the door on the Sabbath won't even indirectly startle an electric motor into life, which would be a violation of the religious law.

That would be okay, I guess, if they kept it to themselves, but they are still family, and they show up at funerals to criticize the rest of us. And the worst of it is that none of us ever knows quite what to say.

What Barry said was that if this was how they held shovels, he understood why Jews were never much good at farming. Not all that funny, maybe, but at that moment it had a certain effect, so that Clare, Lois' younger sister, began giggling and couldn't stop. This was awkward out there under the tent at the open grave. Stephen, our cousin, who was staring down at his mother's coffin, looked up and just barely kept from asking what in hell was going on. One could hardly blame him.

Back at the apartment that had been Aunt Mollie's, we all reassembled to sit with Stephen for a while and wait at least for the evening prayers. There were the inevitable platters of cold cuts and an array of unopened liquor bottles on the sideboard. Probably Lois' doing—one of her many good works that are less endearing than they would be if they weren't so calculated, such predictable consequences of her piety. On the other hand, spontaneous kindness can be unreliable.

Barry looked at the bottles, opened one, and told us about his latest project, a scheme to import vodka from Israel. The idea was that it would be a "light" vodka, because Jews are light drinkers. But the trouble was that if it's less than seventy proof, there has to be some awkward word, like *Diluted,* which has to appear in letters as large as anything else on the label.

Barry, a big supporter of Israel, is the richest guy in the family. He is also something of a clown. He announced to us that the best part of his new project was the name he had devised for the product: Massada.

Clare laughed. Stephen roused himself to suggest a slogan that could be very catchy. "Massada Vodka—Everybody falls for it!"

Lois thought this was sacrilegious, an insult to the memory of martyrs.

I wasn't much worried about the memory of martyrs. I worried more that Barry could drop a bundle on a product that had no chance, not with *Diluted* in big letters on the label. I poured myself a little Scotch and thought about vodka. I wondered aloud why all vodkas seem to come from northern countries, from cold countries. "There isn't any Italian vodka," I said, "or Greek or Spanish vodka. Whatever it is, that's why Israeli vodka sounds odd."

"They have grapes," Stephen suggested. "It's easier to make wine than it is to make whiskey or vodka."

I walked around the apartment and wondered who would take care of Aunt Mollie's plants now. I hadn't cried at the funeral or at the cemetery and I wasn't weeping now, but for the first time that day it was a struggle. And it was too absurd to talk about. I remembered how I had given away my mother's plants to her next-door neighbor, who had taken them to the vestry of her church where, presumably, conceivably, they may still be thriving. Are there plant orphanages? Could Barry make another killing with an idea like that?

It was displacement, of course. I could figure that out for myself. But while figuring these things out can help, it doesn't make grief go away.

I finished my drink, got some water from the sink, and poured a little into each of the pots on the windowsill. The begonias, Christmas cactus, jade plants, and Swedish ivy were languishing in the sunshine and trying stupidly to assert not only their individual existences but some more general idea of life itself.

I hung around—we all did—until the evening prayers so that Stephen could say Kaddish with the official quorum of ten that seems to be required to get God's flighty attention. Perhaps He is distracted by all those sparrows. It was not the moment, though, to try to lift Stephen's spirits with such banter, even though that was exactly what he and I had always done at these family occasions. From boyhood, such dumb jokes had been our way of fighting boredom and staying sane. They were our signatures. But this occasion was serious, almost overwhelming. We all read together the Hebrew prayers that only Lois and Morris understood or got much benefit from. But what else was there to do?

Afterwards I hugged Stephen and told him I'd be in touch. If he needed anything, he should call.

A couple of months went by. We had lunch together in the city a few times, but then we missed some connections. Stephen had to go down to Texas, I think, on business, and then I was away myself for a while. When I got back, it would cross my mind every so often that I ought to call him, and I meant to, but I also figured that if he needed me, he would call. Besides, what is there for cousins to say to one another? What is there for anyone to say to anyone at such a time? That the ache eventually dulls? That's a more or less unwelcome truth each of us must discover for himself.

When he did call, it was about Aunt Mollie's will. Apparently all the witnesses were also dead, and somebody had to appear to verify one of their signatures. My mother had been one of the witnesses—my father had drawn the will—and I could do this. I could also swear that, to my knowledge, Aunt Mollie had not had any other children, legitimate or illegitimate—a perfectly absurd suggestion, but one about which the surrogate's court of Rockland County needed some reassurance. I asked if this couldn't be done by affidavit, and Stephen admitted that, yes, it probably could. But I'd have to go to a county clerk's office to swear to what his lawyer would have to draw up, which would take time and cost money. It was, he said, a pain in the neck either way, but if I came up to New York, he could drive me up to New City, and then we could have dinner together. We could also stop at Aunt Mollie's apartment— he was still clearing out some things—and I could keep him company.

"Sure," I said, remembering what that terrible job was like. "I'll be glad to. Is Friday okay?"

It was as good as any other day. I took the train to New York, met Stephen in his office, and then walked with him to a construction site where he'd made a week-to-week deal to park his somewhat beat-up Toyota from which the radio had long ago been stolen. He kept a small boom-box in the trunk with a plastic case of cassettes. He let me choose what we'd play on the trip. There was no Mozart; the best I could find was Benny Goodman, which he thought was amusing.

It was a gentle spring day, so even the commercial stretches of New Jersey through which we drove looked less ugly than usual. We traded bits of family news. There wasn't much, except that Barry had decided not to go ahead with his Israeli vodka project. Stephen railed some at Lois, who, for all her aggressive piety, had found few occasions to visit during the last days of her aunt's illness. Stephen seemed to be recovering well enough, I thought.

We arrived at New City, and I swore to what was obviously the truth, wavering in my feelings between sadness and annoyance that Stephen and I were being put through this nonsense for so modest an estate. For a few thousand dollars, what claimants were going to present themselves as long-lost heirs?

When we went back to Aunt Mollie's apartment, I saw

that all those plants of hers had died. Like the household servants of old Chinese emperors who were buried alive when the emperor died. There was a dripping noise from the bathroom, from a worn washer in the tub. The air was stale, and the rooms were cluttered with boxes Stephen had left on his last foray, when he had reached that point where he could stand it no longer, had dropped what he was doing, and had driven away.

All the liquor bottles were gone but one, which still had a couple of fingers of Canadian that Stephen hadn't thought worth taking. Or had left deliberately for his next visit. We rummaged in the kitchen, found a couple of those glasses that sour cream comes in, rinsed them out, and poured the last of the whiskey. On one of his earlier visits, Stephen had unplugged the refrigerator, so there was no ice. We drank English fashion, which was fine.

"So what are you going to do with this place?" I asked. "Sell it? Move in? You could commute to New York."

"No, I'll probably sell it," he said. "I'd been thinking of hanging onto it through the summer, though. I figure I can use it on weekends. There's a pool down there. But I don't know. All the blue-haired ladies go down with their chairs and sit there. They never go in. They just sit there."

"So? What's the matter with that?"

"It's okay," he said, "but I'm not sure it's how I want to spend my summer. Besides, one of them stole all of Mom's earrings. All the good ones, anyway. It's annoying."

"They took care of her when she was sick. They came to see her, at least. They were friendly enough," I said, not to defend them, but to try to make him feel better about it.

"I know. That's what I tell myself. And I would have been happy to give them the earrings. But it's different, somebody just coming in and taking them like that."

"Yes," I agreed, "it is."

We emptied our glasses. Stephen put them on the old Rubbermaid drain on the sink. "You want something?" he offered abruptly. "Something that was hers? Something she touched?"

"Sure," I said. "That'd be nice."

"Go ahead. Pick something out."

I looked around. There wasn't a whole lot to pick from. Aunt Mollie and Uncle Paul had lived comfortably enough, I suppose, but they hadn't cared much about objects. I could not see anything that looked right, that had anything personal or distinctive about it except, of course, for the pictures of Stephen that hung on their walls or stood on the heavy pieces of Grand Rapids furniture with which they had put up or made do, settling for them or perhaps hardly even noticing them. And Stephen was there in the flesh. I did see a pretty teapot that Aunt Mollie had left out for show and asked about that.

"I brought that back from London for her," Stephen said. "She didn't use it really."

Did he want it for himself? Or was he trying to steer me to something that had been more closely associated with his mother? Either way, my course was clear. I looked elsewhere. I began to worry that there might not be anything suitable and that either Stephen or I or both of us might be dreadfully embarrassed. Should I ask him to find something for me? I went into the bedroom, thinking there might be a nice bedside clock. A perfume atomizer. A letter opener. Or some little box she'd kept jewelry in. Anything at all.

It was all insignificant, unremarkable, absolutely impersonal junk, of minimal interest even to those archaeologists who might happen upon it after the nuclear winter came to an end. At last, on a small hanging shelf in the living room, I found a fluted Royal Worcester demitasse with a spray of small pink flowers on it. "How about this?" I asked.

"Sure," he said. "I don't know where she got that. It was always here. Anyway, it was hers."

172

"That's fine," I said. "Thanks."

We found some newspaper to wrap it in, and I carried it carefully out of the apartment and down the hall to the elevator. The hallway smelled faintly of some chemical approximation of flowers—the kind of perfume exterminators add to their poisons. I remembered the homelier but more honest smell of cooked cabbage that had hung in the hallway of their old apartment in the Bronx before they moved up to Spring Valley.

In the lobby, we went to the mailbox alcove. Aunt Mollie's was crammed full, and Stephen struggled to extract from it fistfuls of mail.

"You ought to leave a forwarding address."

"It's complicated," he said. "I mean, what I should have done was forge Mom's name and send in a card. That would have worked. But I called them, so they know she's dead. But now they need proof of it—a copy of the death certificate and God knows what else. I'll have to come up during the week with all that stuff. One of these days I'll get around to it, I guess."

"It's a pain in the ass," I condoled.

There was a back stairway leading down to the basement and out to the parking lot behind the building, and Stephen led the way through that shortcut. He had the mail, bills mostly, and I was carrying my little cup.

As we approached the door to the parking lot, we passed another couple coming into the building, a man in his sixties carrying bags of groceries, and his wife, a little younger, with one bag and, in her free hand, a heavy set of keys. What struck me about them, even before they spoke, was how they were both scowling fiercely, although quite possibly the overhead light bulb in its protective wire cage may have exaggerated to some extent their unpleasant expressions.

But it wasn't the lighting. They were really annoyed.

"You wouldn't be the owner of that blue Toyota, would you?" the man asked us, jutting his jaw forward as if he might bite one of us.

"No, no," Stephen said. "Mine is the silver Mercedes."

"Some son of a bitch is in our parking place," the man groused.

"No consideration!" the woman complained, shaking her head. "There are visitors' spaces, clearly designated."

"Some people!" Stephen said, as if commiserating.

They trudged on past, and once the door closed behind us, Stephen explained to me that there was an assigned space for each apartment. Aunt Mollie's space was nearly in the middle of Kansas, but that hadn't bothered her. She hadn't had a car. "I just park anywhere," he said. "There are always plenty of spaces. But they have meetings and worry about things like this. Could you believe her? 'There are visitors' spaces, clearly designated.' "

We drove back to New York and had dinner there. Then Stephen dropped me off at Penn Station. I watched his blue Toyota disappear down Seventh Avenue and, cradling the little fluted cup, made my way to the train.

I got it home all right and put it away in the breakfront, where it keeps company with a lot of other expensive stuff I don't use very often: the Baccarat caviar server, the Imari bowl, the good things we can never really claim as our own. Unless we break them, they will survive us, float serenely from one household to the next, pass gracefully through the hands of knowing dealers, and only appreciate through each transaction. All we really own is the junk, the sour cream glasses, the stuff that, at our deaths, will be given away or thrown out, the modest objects that will languish and die, like those plants.

I heard this week that Stephen finally sold the apartment and is going to buy his own place in Brooklyn Heights, which is fine and makes sense. I wished him luck, of course. He's well rid of Aunt Mollie's Spring Valley place, as he was tough enough to see all along. There are no assigned spots. One parks where one can, as Jews should have learned generations ago, however they hold their shovels.

What Aunt Mollie touched, of course, was Stephen, and I think of him, of Stephen and his mother, every time a silver Mercedes passes by.